ONE DAY...
THIS DAY!

Bless You

Cheryl Patton-Bronson

4 Your Spirit Productions
P.O. Box 201718
Chicago, IL 60620-1718

One Day…This Day!

Some Scripture quotations were taken from the HOLY BIBLE
NEW LIVING TRANSLATION
Copyright © 1996, 2004. Used by permission of Tyndale House Publishers, Inc., Wheaton Illinois 60189. All rights reserved.

Unless otherwise identified, Scripture quotations are from the Comparative Study Bible, Revised Edition. Copyright © 1999 by the Zondervan Corporation. The translations used for this book are from the:

NEW INTERNATIONAL VERSION
The Holy Bible, New International Version®
Copyright© 1973, 1978, 1984 by International Bible Society

NASB UPDATE
New American Standard Bible
Copyright © 1960, 1962, 1963, 1968, 1971, 1973, 1975, 1977, 1995 by the Lockman Foundation, A Corporation Not for Profit, La Habra, CA
All rights reserved

AMPLIFIED BIBLE, EXPANDED EDITION
Copyright © 1987 by The Zondervan Corporation and the Lockman Foundation
All rights reserved

This book is a work of fiction. Names, characters, places, and incidents either are products of the author's imagination or are used fictitiously, and any resemblance to actual persons, living or dead, business establishments, events, or locales is entirely coincidental.

Editor: Regina Carver (copyediting_help@yahoo.com)
Cover Design: Cheryl Bronson

ISBN: 978-0-6151-4908-0

Library of Congress Control Number: 2007905882

For more information about the author, this book, and additional writings, visit
www.4yourspirit.com or e-mail the author directly:
cbronson@4yourspirit.com

DEDICATION

I dedicate this book to my wonderful brother, Steven Eugene Patton and my dad, Billy Michael Anthony Cooke. Even though you both are no longer here to encourage and support me, your memory remains in and with me. You pushed me to go on and finish the fight. I love and miss you so much. You are my inspiration. One day, your lives will be written, here on earth, as it is in Heaven, so that others may be blessed by your struggles, your love, and your visions.

Peace *G*

AML AML
(All My Love, All My Life)

ACKOWLEDGMENTS

This book was inspired by my God, my Holy Father in Heaven and I could not have accomplished this without daily prayers. I was guided by and wrapped in His Word throughout this entire process. If I did not pray first, He would not give me one word to type in this book. So first and foremost I acknowledge My Father, which art in Heaven, who is always in my mind, my heart and my soul. My prayers have always been, 'To You God, and only You, do I give all the glory, all the honor and all the praise. And I thank You Father, for... *'My Everything'*.

I would like to acknowledge two wonderful people who were monumental in my decision to become a writer; Pastor Earl and Clarice Grandberry. God used you to place the Word of God in my heart, to keep me faithful in my prayer life and in my studying, and to show me by example what a relationship with God is all about. It was through you that God pulled out my gifts and I thank you two for being my spiritual leaders during our season of fellowship. The gift which you've sparked in me, God has nurtured, developed, and perfected, so that it may now be shared with others for His glory. Mother Clarice, you are the best! No matter what, thank you for all the love.

A lot of love and support was also given to me throughout the years from so many other people in my life who I have to say are my biggest fans. Some of them are wrapped a little too tight and some aren't wrapped at all, but I gotta love 'em. So, before you read on, take a moment of silence and pray for my peoples for they know not what they do, but I thank God for them everyday. Okay, you ready? (MOMENT OF SILENCE)... Thank you.

Regina R. Patton – my mom, who thinks I can do no wrong. Boy, do I love you for that, but I do have some issues. Yeah, I know that's hard to believe, but I do. Thank you for your constant prayers, support, love, rebuke, discipline, guidance and don't let me leave out finances...throughout my life. God put together an excellent team when He made us mother and daughter. I hope to continue that wonderful example with my daughter, Danielle as well.

Herman Ousley, Jr., a good friend, who feels as though he must read and critique everything I write, even when I'm not finish. You've encouraged me all along the way and I thank you for that. I talk about you and give you a hard time, but it's all in fun. I want you to remember that I'll forever cherish your friendship and support. May God bless you tremendously for being such a good friend.

My girlfriend, my sparring partner, Sharon Buchanan (Shay Shay), who never missed a play I wrote, directed and produced, now that's love. You've always been patient with me and never looked down on me or said one negative word against me *(that*

I know of), in spite of my forgetfulness. We may not get together like we want to, but please know that you're always on my mind and in my prayers. I appreciate the role you play in my life. Just keep pressing forward towards the mark, because in your *press*, God will *bless*. Luv you.

I send big-time love to my posse, Dacia Dixon, Audrey Hendricks-Afari, and Lisa Taylor-Buckhanan. It's such a blessing to be able to have more than one best friend. Dacia, you came into my life at a time when I truly needed someone strong to hold me up. You've held me up many times, when I thought I wouldn't make it. You've supported all of my endeavors, and there were many. You've helped me to grow and taught me to love unconditionally, from your example. You've also shown me true, unconditional friendship, love and support. I know no one who's as giving and as loving as you are. Thank you for being my friend for life. I love you much.

I send so much love to Audrey, who happens to live far away. Well, you're not that far but far enough. You were my first best friend ever. Even though you're around 4 states away, I've felt your love and support all the way from Arlington, Texas. You're there for me 100% of the time, encouraging me. No matter what, I can always depend on you to be there. We became friends in first grade and were separated for twelve years when I moved away. God brought us back together, stronger than ever and nothing or no one shall ever separate us again; for this friendship is of God. I truly praise God for the many contributions you've made in my life. Our experiences together were and are priceless and I pray we have many more. It just doesn't get any better than this.

And then there's Lisa, the special one. While growing up you were so… *busy* (posse girls, you know what I mean). You're the one no one ever thought would be a powder keg for the Kingdom, but actually, the… *'busy'* people, are the ones God can use mightily. And He used you to direct me to the place where I needed to go to learn of Him, to be with Him, and to hear from Him. Who would've thunk? ☺ God did! God has ordered our steps and what matters most is the willingness for us to be open to His Word, open to His commands, open to do His will… not our own. You'll always have a special place in my heart. God has a special place in His heart for nobody but you so remember to keep that sweet spot reserved for nobody but Him. You three women have been phenomenal as friends and I thank you from the depth of my heart.

I didn't forget you Kelly Nichelle Brown, my sweet God-daughter. I thank you for providing me your talents of acting, dancing and choreographing in my times of need (which were quite a few) in directing the plays and musical numbers. Remember that *'all good and all perfect gifts are from God' (Jas.1-17)*. Always dedicate and give back to Him what He has given to you. I love you so much and you'll be richly rewarded for all you've done and are doing; just keep God first. I also thank my God-son, Richard Dixon who's never missed a Mother's Day call and gift and always calls just to see if there's anything I need. Those calls are a blessing to me. Keep 'em coming. You're handling your business in college when so many of our youth drop out for whatever reasons. I'm so proud of you and even more proud to be your God-momma.

I must say this, and I know this will catch you by surprise, Michelle Jones, my spiritual sister. We've known each other for a short time but you've had such a powerful influence in my life. I cannot imagine my life without your love, your encouragement, our and spiritual connection. God placed you in my life for the time we had together, to keep us both in balance with His Word. And it worked. Part of the reason for this book is you. God showed you this project way before He revealed it to me. That's why you continued to push me. Chelle, I love you girl.

And then there's Yvette Johnson-Estelle, yeah I know you thought I forgot about you. Never! Remember, *'many who are first shall be last, and the last shall be first' (Mk 10:31).* You've been an inspiration to me from the moment we met in high school. You were always so focused and disciplined and I know that's not always easy to do. You've always been the person that I admired most in my life, all because of your stand in life, your charisma, and your relationship with the Father.

You're such an outstanding and dedicated mom, friend, and woman of God. Girl, you're the bomb. God did a wonderful thing when He put you in my life and I'll be forever grateful to Him. I'll love, honor, cherish and respect you forever.

Other family members and friends, you'll have to wait for the next book. I love you, even though I know you're all pouting right now.

I really need to thank my editor, my coach, my business partner, my friend, Regina Carver. You steered me in the areas I needed to stay focused and make this vision from God into a reality. You were so encouraging, especially in the moments when I broke down, because the burden became so heavy. But you had a Word for me that I'll never forget; Ephesians 3:20 – *Now unto Him that is able to do exceeding abundantly above all that we ask or think, according to the power that worketh in us.* It's so amazing how God places people in your life and you have no clue just how important their role will be. At least we noticed that right away and followed His divine plan for our lives. May God bless you far more abundantly, above all that you could ever imagine, in Jesus name.

Introduction

2Chronicles 7:11-16, 19-20 (NIV)

[11]*When Solomon had finished the temple of the Lord and the royal palace, and had succeeded in carrying out all he had in mind to do in the temple of the Lord and in his own palace,* [12]*the Lord appeared to him at night and said:*

"I have heard your prayer and have chosen this place for myself as a temple for sacrifices.

[13]*When I shut up the Heavens so that there is no rain, or command locusts to devour the land or send a plague among my people,* [14]*if my people, who are called by My Name, will humble themselves and pray and seek My face and turn from their wicked ways, then will I hear from Heaven and will forgive their sin and will heal their land.* [15]*Now My eyes will be open and My ears attentive to the prayers offered in this place.* [16]*I have chosen and consecrated this temple so that My Name may be there forever. My eyes and My heart will always be there...*

[18]*But if you turn away and forsake the decrees and commands I have given you and go off to serve other gods and worship them,* [20]*then I will uproot Israel from my land, which I have given them and will reject this temple I have consecrated for My Name.*

One

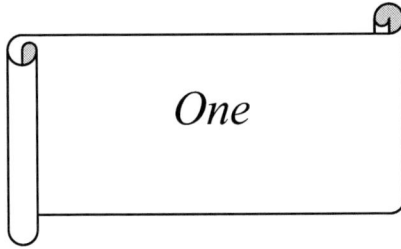

*J*ada Jenkins sat there closely watching him. Once again he had commanded the attention of all who could hear him. She had to pay close attention to him and watch his every move because she never knew when he would call upon her. Sometimes she was so into watching him, that she actually missed what he was saying. She had to learn to balance what was more important; what he was saying or what she would do when he gave the signal. Whenever he would speak, she could tell his speaking was superior by listening to the response of the people. There were times she just repeated what they said to make it look like she was listening. It was not that she didn't believe in what he was saying; she just never wanted to miss her cue. That was so very important to her. As a matter of fact, that was probably the most important thing to her in her life at that moment.

Today, with the exception of him speaking, it was unusually quiet. It was so quiet you could almost hear a pin drop. In reality, an infant was softly cooing in the back where people normally took their young ones when they were a little active or a bit fussy. There had never been a time when infants didn't bellow out at the top of their lungs at least once, causing everyone to look around to see what was going on. But not this day, all the infants were calm. That must've made the mothers real happy since they could concentrate on what he was saying.

There was yet another sound that could be faintly heard in the background other than the babies and the speaker. It was the sleepers. These were the people who weren't there by choice but pressured to come by a loving family member or close friend. But to be fair, some of them had a late night from a long day at work, babies up all night, or a night out at the clubs. The party crew was usually the ones that were more than just sleep; they were actually knocked out. From time to time someone would have to nudge them— but not this day.

Those who were awake were totally engrossed in the words coming forth. He had a way of making you want to walk right up to the devil and slap him in the head for all the mess in your life, even though most of the mess was your own doing. People tend to look for someone to lay the blame on instead of taking a good look in the mirror. Satan was usually the most popular choice for the majority of the blame.

Pastor Jon Devine, senior pastor of the Holy Tabernacle Church had been in this church since he was born. His father was the pastor before him. His grandfather was the pastor before his father. It was actually his great-great grandmother, Mother Alice Devine, who was the very first pastor.

Mother Devine was the matriarch of a large family and she raised them with love, respect, and compassion for others. All this was centered on biblical teachings. She started the church in the basement of their family building with seven other family members who lived there. Eventually all the Devine family members would attend the Bible meetings.

Her true desire was to reach out to any of the poor or unfortunate families in her immediate surroundings. The entire neighborhood knew she genuinely loved and cared about them. They would often visit to hear her words of wisdom, which was usually accompanied with a nice hot meal. Due to her compassionate acts, more than family members began to attend the family Bible meetings and it began to grow and grow. It soon outgrew the family basement and they were in dire need of more space. The elder mothers from the Bible meetings organized a fundraiser to help the growing congregation have funds to either rent or buy their very first church.

A local businessman heard about their work in the community and their desire to have a larger, more organized place of their own. He admired their commitment and determination and made a pledge to triple the amount they raised. Members placed second mortgages on their homes and buildings, cashed in bonds, gave portions of their savings and tithed heavily to the church. Through all this sacrifice from the members and the community, a beautiful church building was built. Seventy-five years later, the ministry was still going strong with a heavy commitment to community outreach, which was the vision God had originally given to Mother Devine.

The problem now was, there hadn't been an increase in membership for a while and Pastor Jon Devine knew he needed to do something different. The first thing he believed he needed to do was change the style of his message. He wanted to reach the people by appealing to their need for deliverance without condemning them. Condemnation and strict rules were some of the ways the church kept the members in line when he was growing up. But this was a new day. People needed to know the truth, the naked truth; the uncompromising truth without feeling judged or put down but yet understanding the consequences of sin. The church had a way of wounding its wounded, not recognizing that the church is nothing but a big spiritual hospital. Everybody, from the pews to the pulpit, had some type of problem, You name it! It was all in the church.

Pastor Devine had to find a way to communicate to the congregation that problems are a part of life's trials. The church was the place for healing all wounds. He wanted them to understand that everyone commit sins, even him! And they all will continue to sin. It was up to him to teach them what they needed to do after committing the sin and most importantly, how to keep from repeating it. This, he believed, would ultimately break some generational curses.

The second thing he needed to do was tie it all in to music. This was an age of music and children, teens, young and old adults, were into it. They each may have had their own style, but they all loved music just the same. Radios, computers, laptops, portable CD players, DVDs, DVRs, IPODs, MP3 players, cell phones, pens, watches, belt buckles, you name it...everyone and everything played music. Music had a way of influencing one's mind, heart and soul. He needed to tap into that phenomenon and add that element to his sermons. In doing this, he would bring music back to what it was originally intended for; *glorifying God*. So Pastor Devine fasted and prayed, until God answered.

The congregation of Holy Tabernacle Church was sitting on the edge of their seats, eyes focused; hanging onto Pastor

Devine's every word. For the past few months, they had been wondering what had gotten into him but they were loving every bit of it.

Pastor Devine moved gracefully across the pulpit; preaching and teaching the Word of God, pounding on the podium for emphasis.

"Now my God is a mighty God. I said my God is a mighty God and a merciful God. I serve a God of justice. A God of righteousness! The God I serve does not force anything on you. He's the God of choice and wants us to know that certain choices bring rewards.

"Now according to the Bible in Deuteronomy, Chapter 28, it says that first you must hear and listen to the voice of God. After you've heard and listened to Him, then you must follow and obey His laws, obey His ways. Then and only then my brothers and sisters, will He put you high over all the nations of the earth.

"Look folks, let me tell you something, my God is giving you the opportunity to put Him first so that He can reward you. In doing this He said all these blessings; did you hear me when I said '*all these blessings*' will be given unto you? How many people feel like being blessed this morning? Look over and tell your neighbor, '*I want all the blessings of God.*'"

The people respond and he continues, "Not only will He bless you, but the blessings will come on you and overtake you! Do you hear what I'm saying to you? Do you know what it's like to be overtaken? Well let me tell you. Overtaken is when you just can't take no more. I said when you just can't take no more; when it's just more than you can handle. Tell me how many want to be blessed with more than you can handle? *Say Amen somebody!*"

The congregation comes to life and responds to his high spirited preaching with a hearty "AMEN".

Pastor continues.

"Now here's where it gets better. If what I already said is just not good enough for you, then hear this. A blessing will come to you in the town where you live—*he bams on the podium.* A blessing will come to the place where you work! A blessing will come from the fruit of your body. A blessing will be on your land and all that you own and will own. You will be blessed walking in the door and blessed walking right back out that door. *Did you hear what I said church?"*

The more he speaks the more the crowd responds. People are starting to stand up leaning forward as if the closer they lean, the better they will be able to hear him. They even exchange glances with each other and nod from time to time in agreement with the pastor.

The entire church choir has risen and Jada notices how they are responding so she stands as well. She's listening more to the response of the audience than the response of the choir, while still looking directly at the Pastor. She glances every now and then at the choir members but she has pretty much trained her ear towards the congregation. This is not an easy task, just a necessary task. She really can't feel the power of his words because her concentration is more on his body movement. The response of the people will let her know how she needs to carry out her part in all of this. She needs to feel the pulse of the people. She glances about and notices that all the people standing respond to Pastor Devine with *"Yeah"* every time he ends a sentence.

Once Pastor has realized he has their complete attention, he hits them with a *"Can I get an Amen somebody?"* On this, more than half the church is standing and responding. Even those who were trying to sleep are awakened due to all the interaction between the pastor and his congregation. They all respond with a resounding *"AMEN."*

Pastor Jon Devine continues.

"His blessings will be on you in the land which He has given you. And all the peoples—*he bams on the podium*—I said all the peoples of the earth will see that the name of the Lord is on you, covering you. They will see that you're blessed. They will go in fear of you. You see, God will have your enemies afraid of you. He said He will make your enemies your foot stool. How many of you want to rest your feet on the back of the ones that oppress you? The ones that come against you in your ministry for the Father; the ones that mistreat, misuse and abuse you." Pastor pauses, "but know this saints, in spite of what they do to you, you still have to love those same folks. See, you are to hate that spirit; hate the sins, but love the people. Amen?"

"Amen!" is their response.

"That was for somebody up in here. I can feel you pulling on my spirit. But I can't be side tracked this morning! Now let me go on. He said in His Word that He will make you the head and not the tail. I said the head and not the tail. I'm talking about a CEO; I'm talking about a president of a company! I'm talking about the owner and operator of your own business. Can I get an, *Amen* from somebody who wants to be the head, a leader of man, and not the tail, a follower of man?"

On this note, the whole place gets fired up. People are jumping up and down at the thought of being in charge, running their own businesses and even being the head of someone else's business. The thought of having that type of charge and power has set them into a spiritual frenzy. It's as if for the first time in their lives, they believe what Pastor Devine is saying could actually happen in their lives.

"But oh let me tell you my people, there's another side to this story. There's yet another choice that you can make. God wants to give you the blessings, but you must first acknowledge Him so that He may direct you in order to do His

21

will. If your choice is to not give ear to His voice, not to do His will, not to walk in the example that Jesus gave; then curses, I said curses will come on you and overtake you!"

Maxine stands with both arms raised and a serious look on her face. She yells from the choir stand "That's right Pastor! You go 'head on and preach!" His energy level increases just a little bit more at this outburst of encouragement as he seems to feed off her words.

"Now listen to me people, I'm not here to scare you. God's purpose is not to scare you. His purpose is for you to understand the consequences of your choices, of your actions, of your decisions. So here we are, 'bout to be overtaken again. But now, you're about to get exactly what you worked for… but really didn't plan on.

"Disobedience to God's Word can cause you to be cursed where you live, cursed where you work. The fruit of your body and the fruit of your land can be cursed! You can be cursed when you come in and cursed when you go out. Curses can come on you and on your seed, to be a sign and a wonder *fah-e-vah!* Did you hear me saints? I said did you hear me say *fah-e-vah.* And this is all because you would not give honor! You would not give heed! You would not give your ear to the voice of the Lord, worshipping Him gladly, being obedient with joy in your hearts! I said, with true joy in your hearts!

"But let me tell somebody, I serve a Mighty God. I said I serve a Mighty God. I serve a Wondrous God. I serve an Awesome God. My God is a Merciful God. I serve a God of justice, a God of righteousness! A Forgiving God! The God of choice. The Only God, the Great Jehovah! The God that sent His Son named Jesus, to die for all your unrighteousness—*he bams on the podium*—for all my unrighteousness—*he bams on the podium again.* So that the curse of the law might be broken. For Christ has rescued us from the curse pronounced by the law. When He hung on that old rugged cross, He took upon Himself the curse for our wrongdoings; for He said in His Word, cursed is He who is hung upon the tree. For now we're entitled to the blessings of Abraham. For Jesus has taken upon Himself all your migraines, all your arthritis, all your cancer, your HIV, your Herpes, your backaches, your headaches, your heartaches, all your trials, all your tribulations! *Can I get an Amen somebody?*"

"*AMEN*" they yell.

"He said in His Word—*he bams on the podium*—I said He said in His Word, I've set before you blessings and curses, and I've set before you life and death, therefore *choose LIFE that you may LIVE church!* Let me say it one more time, I said *choose LIFE that you may LIVE!*"

With the exception of the few people wiping the sleep out their eyes wondering what's really going on, Pastor Devine has been able to inspire the entire congregation. People continue jumping up and down waving their hands in the air in agreement with the Word. They respond to his words of choosing life.

They all repeat in unison after him, "*LIVE!*"

Those who were asleep have now completely awakened and join in with those who are standing to become a part of this thunderous call and response.

Pastor comes back with "I said *LIVE*"

"*LIVE!*" the congregation yells once again.

This exchange goes on and on; back and forth until the pastor changes up on them with "*Can I get an Amen somebody?*" as he bams on the podium. They all obediently respond with a thunderous "*AMEN!*"

By this time, the musicians have moved to their instruments instinctively playing along with the pastor and worshippers' exchange of words. The music in the background mixed in with the pastor's words, seems to add another level of excitement and self-examination amongst the congregation.

Pastor comes back at them with "Love the Lord your God! I said Love the Lord your God that you may *What Church?*"

"*LIVE!*" the congregation responds.

"That you may *What?*"

"*LIVE!*"

Pastor Devine claps his hands and says in a powerful and loud voice *"Hallelujah to The Almighty God! He Wants You To Live Church, Live!"*

The congregation at Holy Tabernacle Church is yelling and shouting praises to their Almighty God. The musicians strike a chord which incites the people into a more orchestrated praise. That's when it happens; the moment has finally come. Pastor Devine gives a subtle nod to his Minister of Music who in turn gives the nod to Jada. Jada doesn't need the nod from the Minister of Music, but waits out of respect. Sometimes the minister misses Pastor's nod so Jada must always be watching to make sure she doesn't.

Jada Jenkins, the very beautiful and talented lead singer of the Holy Tabernacle Church Gospel Choir, methodically acknowledges their nods and slowly walks up to the microphone, allowing herself to get into the spirit of the music as she prepares to join in with the musicians. Then perfectly, on cue as always, just the way Pastor Devine wants it, she lets out such a melodious sound that it completely moves the people. The very sound of her wonderful and powerful voice takes them away. Their heads seem to swell as the words and the notes magically flow from her mouth to their ears. What she sings, and the conviction in which she sings, makes them feel as if they can relate to every word, every phrase, and every feeling.

She knows the effect her voice has on them; the goose bumps they feel whenever she sings. They can never seem to hold back the emotion that comes forth when she sings. The songs Pastor selects for her have become the perfect message for the sermon preached, or the situation you just so happen to be going through. Jada bellows out strong, precise and perfectly pitched notes that are matched by no other singer in the church. And probably unmatched by any of the professional singers in the Gospel or secular realm. Jada feeds off their emotions as she just carries them away to a whole 'nother level of praise and worship of the Almighty God.

Two

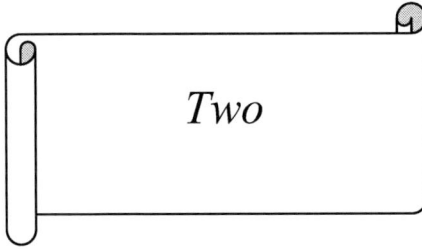

All that shouting and praising worked up a heck of an appetite for the members of the Holy Tabernacle Church. Che Che's Place, located across from Washington Park, was just a few blocks away from the church. It was the perfect eatery for hungry folks on Sunday after a fired up, energetic church service.

Actually, Che Che's Place was the place to go no matter what the day of the week or how hungry you were. It was well known for its quaint atmosphere, affordable prices, and friendly service. Well, the friendly service could be tested from time to time. It was based on how you approached Ms. Che Che. If you came right, she came back right; you came wrong and Ms. Che Che would come back at you with a vengeance. But in order for that to happen, you really had to be dead wrong.

More importantly, Ms. Che Che's food was the best in Chi-town. She didn't play when it came to cooking. She could cook absolutely anything and her specialty was soul food with a kick of spiciness. You could order your meal mild or spicy, but if you picked spicy, you better hold on to your seat 'cause you were 'bout to be in for the ride of your life. Her spicy fried cabbage was one of the favorites on the menu. Every time you took a forkful, you just knew you had died and gone to Heaven sitting right next to the Father, the Son and the Holy Spirit; and all three of them had a plate too. It was pretty obvious that God gave Ms. Che Che the gift of cooking. Not only did He give her that gift that was matched by no other, He must have hand delivered every one of those recipes to her.

Ms. Che Che's Place was definitely the hot spot on Sunday and sometimes the line would be wrapped around the block. No matter how crowded it was Ms. Che Che always had a table available for her three favorite girls, Jada Jenkins, Trina Hendricks and Maxine Taylor. The girls met there every Sunday after morning service and at least two to three days out of the week. They were considered regulars, and not just any regulars but the big-time regulars with big-time privileges. People used to be a little upset and complained when the girls walked right up and got a table, but Ms. Che Che didn't care and didn't play that. Once she got finished reading whoever complained, she reminded them how they were more than welcome to leave and never come back. Most times, they would shut right up and never say anything again, at least about those girls. Some things just weren't worth complaining about.

On this day, Trina happened to be the first to get there. She went directly to their reserved table located in the back dining area, right next to the kitchen entrance. Ms. Che Che waved to Trina with a spoon in her hand as she passed the kitchen. Ms. Che Che dipped the spoon into the pot, scooping up some collard greens and came out to the table already set up for the three girls.

"How's my girl doing today?" She placed the spoon up to Trina's mouth for a taste test.

"I'm fine Ms. Che Che," Trina said trying to eat every leaf of the collard greens on the spoon. "Oh my God! Ms. Che Che, this is the bomb!"

"I thought you might like this." Ms. Che Che dabbed at Trina's mouth with the napkin, laughing at her greediness and then gave her a big hug. "Where's the rest of your posse? I know they haven't gone somewhere else. I made a special plate for that Jada. I heard she tore the church up today! I hate I couldn't make service."

"She was awwright... I need to stop lying. She was the bomb! But then, she's always the bomb!" Trina starts to pout. "I hope she ain't the only one with a special plate."

"Oh hush girl and sit down. You know I got you covered."

Trina sat down licking her lips. From the smell in the kitchen to the taste in her mouth, her stomach was growling big time.

"Jada and Maxine are on their way," Trina said. "Since they're in the choir and doing some stuff for Minister Peaches, I came ahead so you wouldn't think we weren't going to show up. But I don't have to wait for them Ms. Che Che, you could hook me up right now."

"You a little hungry huh?"

"Ms. Che Che, I'm starving!"

"Good, now wait for the girls!" Ms. Che Che sashayed her way back into the kitchen.

Luckily for Trina's stomach, Jada and Maxine were walking through the door. Maxine headed right for the table, she was ready to eat. Jada on the other hand was being stopped by many of the people in the restaurant who recognized her from church.

"Good job today Jada," came from one of the ladies standing in line.

"You really blessed me," was the comment from another.

"Girl I didn't know you had it in you like that," from yet another member of the church.

This went on and on as Jada thanked the people she walked by for their words of encouragement. In fact, she was used to this. Lately, whenever they had a service and she sang, she was treated like a celebrity. And so far, ever since she first sang in the church choir, she has never missed singing at a service, concert or any other engagement.

"Jada come on!" Trina yelled from the back of the restaurant. "You know Ms. Che Che is not going to feed us unless we're here sitting together. Maxie and I are starving girl, so come on!"

Jada finally made her way to the table and sat down. "I had to be nice, plus did you hear all the stuff people were saying to me about the service today?"

Maxine replied, "Forget about you for just one moment Ms. Superstar. Did you hear all the stuff Pastor was saying? I must say, he got down today. Matter of fact, he's been off the hook for the past couple of months."

"Yeah, you're right. Pastor Devine sure can preach," Jada said.

Trina jumps in. "Well I heard it too, but so what. I don't understand what all the fuss is about. All preachers are alike. *Boooring*!!!" Trina begins to mimic Pastor Devine. "*Live Church! Did You Hear Me? I Said Live Church! Live!!*" Jada and Maxine laugh at Trina's portrayal of the pastor.

Maxine nudges Trina. "Girl, you crazy! But that message he preached about living and dying, blessings and curses was pretty powerful whether or not you want to admit it."

"Look," Trina says. "The only thing I'll admit to is I already know how to live; *Sex, Drugs and Alcohol.* I also already know how to die; *Sex, Drugs and Alcohol.*" She hops up; does a little dance and yells out, "*Heyyyyy!*"

Ms. Che Che comes out with their plates, places them on the table and pushes Trina back down in her seat. "Girl if you don't sit your little hot self down. I got just what it takes to simmer you down. Can't nothing come up in here hotter than me or my food."

The girls look at each other and laugh.

"Well, Ms. Che Che," Jada said, "I think your menu is going to have a run for its money if you're going to compare it with Ms. Hot Mama here."

Trina jumps up again and bends over and acts like she's lighting a match off her derriere. Everyone laughs, even Ms. Che Che.

"Now I know you crazy," Maxine says shaking her head.

Ms. Che Che leaves still laughing, throwing her hands in the air like there's no hope for Trina. Trina flops back down saying, "Hey Jada, I know another way to live and not die."

"And what way is that?"

Trina scoots closer to Jada and tries to block out Maxine.

"There's a party tonight at the Wild Card. You should come and go with me. They gon' be jukin' all night long." She gets up again and starts to dance as if she's at the club. "Better yet," she continues as she sits back down, "I heard they have a new live band down there. I gotta go and hear that."

Jada's eyes light up. "Yeah! But guess—"

"Now Jada," Maxine interrupts. "You're the lead singer in the choir and there's a musical later on this afternoon."

"I know about the musical. I wouldn't miss that for the world. Plus Pastor Devine would kill me if I didn't come. But what—"

"Well that's not the only problem. Getting out of church and going to a club is hypocritical, don't you think?"

Jada throws her hand up in Maxine's face. "Why you keep interrupting me! You're not the only one who has something to say here! Now what's so wrong with me going to a club? I can go to church and a club. That's not being a hypocrite."

"I know you joking. The Spirit was all up in you this morning and you just tore the church up singing. You almost knocked everybody down shouting and praising God. I'm sure the Spirit will be riding high again this afternoon, finishing up what was started this morning. So after being in the Spirit all day, you gon' leave the presence of the Lord to go to a club where nothing in there has anything to do with Him."

"What you saying Maxie; I'm not saved because I want to go to the club? Whether you want to believe it or not, I can be saved and still get my party on with my girl Trina here. God ain't said nothing 'bout *Thou Shalt Not Party at the Clubs!"*

That's your choice not to club, not mine. I'm not all stuffy like you."

Jada and Maxine are more into the conversation than the good food. The conversation has not slowed Trina down one bit. Jada and Maxine are slowly eating and picking at their food whereas Trina has not missed a bite of food with her steady rhythm. In between bites, she takes food off Jada and Maxie's plate.

Trina nudges Maxine. "You think you gon' eat your fried cabbage? Ms. Che Che gave me collard greens. When you mix the greens with the cabbage, the taste is unbelievable."

Maxine waves her fork at Trina to take what she wants and then looks up at Jada.

"Jada, I'm not trying to stop you, I'm trying to paint you a picture. I believe you can walk this walk and still have fun. I want you to have fun because Christians do have fun. We just have to be sure the focus and purpose to what we do is on God because we represent God. That's part of our Godly character. And yes I do believe you're saved, I just don't think you live…like you should sometimes."

Jada pauses for a minute and looks down at her plate. "Then you really not gon' like my news."

Trina finally looks up from her plate. "What news?"

"I don't know if Maxie is ready for this."

"Girl don't pay Maxie no mind, you know she just holy holy. What's your news?"

Maxine turns toward Trina. "Why you gotta call me holy holy all the time? I'm just like you." Maxie thinks about that statement and looks Trina up and down. "Well now that I think about it... I'll take that back, I'll be holy holy."

Jada and Maxine start laughing.

"That's not funny," Trina says. She turns to Maxie, "You ain't funny! Now hush and let's see what Jada's talkin' about? Jada, what's your news?"

Jada tries to stop laughing. "Okay, okay, let me control myself. You two are too funny."

"Girl, stop stalling! What's your news?" Trina asked.

Jada pauses for a minute.

"Alright, here it comes," she says. "You know that new live band you were talking about at the Wild Card?"

Trina looks at her wild eyed, "Yeah, I heard they gon' be the bomb."

"Everything is the bomb to you," Jada said. She puts her head down and whispers. "You're looking at the lead singer for the band."

"What you say?" Trina asked. "Girl, speak up and don't play with me!"

Jada slowly raises her head. "You're looking at the new lead singer for that new band *Eklyptic* performing tonight."

Jada softly claps her hands in excitement hoping the others will join in.

"Girl shut up! You lyin'!" Trina said.

"No I'm not lying. I needed some extra money and I heard they were having auditions so I went and auditioned. They called me back and asked me to perform with them. I've been rehearsing for a couple of weeks now."

Trina starts to scream. Everyone in the restaurant looks their way. Even Ms. Che Che comes running out of the kitchen.

"What's going on here? Is the food too hot?"

Trina is so excited she doesn't even notice Ms. Che Che. "Girl you're kiddin'! I know you kiddin'! Hell naw!" She looks up and sees Ms. Che Che. "Oops, I'm sorry Ms. Che Che." Trina turns back towards Jada. "Heckie naw! Girl, I'm there! Now you know I'm there. I am so there and I'm so happy for you, too." Trina pulls Jada over and starts hugging her. "Girl, this is going to be the bomb!"

Ms. Che Che looks around the table at the girls. "Happy for what…for whom? Y'all better not leave me in suspense. What's going on here?"

"Ms. Che Che, dig this," Trina said. "Jada will be singing with that new band Eklyptic at the Wild Card tonight. Can you believe it?" Trina pulls out her cell phone and starts dialing numbers not even waiting for Ms. Che Che to respond. "Now let me call some people to have them meet us there. I'm gon' have everybody and their momma in the club cheering you on. Girl, you better be good. Don't make me look bad. But then again, I really don't have to tell you that. You the bomb!" Trina begins to talk on the cell phone ignoring everyone in the room.

Ms. Che Che slightly folds her arms, leans against Maxine's chair and looks at Jada. All this time, Maxine has stayed quiet trying to find the right words to say, while Trina runs her mouth at a hundred miles a minute. Maxine and Ms. Che Che exchange glances.

"Okay… what about the musical?" Maxine finally asks still trying to find the right things to say.

"Girl I ain't crazy! I'm gon' be there and then we'll leave and go straight to the club. I'll bring my clothes with me. Just wait 'til you see the outfit I put together."

Jada looks up at Ms. Che Che still leaning there with her arms folded. Jada quickly turns her head away and takes a bite of food before it gets too cold. She's a little afraid of what Ms. Che Che is thinking.

Maxine slightly leans back from Jada. "You know, if that's what you want, who am I to say anything. All I can say is just remember you represent Holy Tabernacle Church."

"I know Maxie. I know. I would never do anything that would make my church or my pastor look bad."

"And you think this doesn't? What do you think Pastor would say if he heard about one of his singers singing in a club?"

Ms. Che Che finally speaks up. "Listen to your sister, Jada. She's telling you right."

"This isn't about right or wrong, it's about me. It's about me making some extra money and possibly making a name for myself. This could be my big break. And anyway, who gon' tell Pastor? You!"

"Who are you talking to like that?" Ms. Che Che raises her voice at Jada. "Don't you dare get besides yourself over you singing a few notes in a club! You ain't all that! I can see you are starting to smell yourself already."

"Ms. Che Che, I was talking to Maxine… not you. You've been a mother to me, especially since my mom died. I would never disrespect you like that. You two are misunderstanding what's going on here. I just don't think Pastor would have a problem with this. What's so wrong about me singing in a night club? I can sing Gospel music at church and sing secular inspirational music at the club as long as it's in good taste. I'm not hurting anybody."

Ms. Che Che sits down in the empty chair next to Jada.

"Actually, you are," Ms. Che Che says. "You are hurting everybody who hears or knows about you singing and shouting on Sunday and then turn around singing and dancing at the club. You're showing the people we're trying to reach that it's okay to be a *Saint* at church and an *Ain't* everywhere else. You're sending mixed signals. This is one of the main reasons for the confusion now in the Christian faith. I'm not trying to be preachy, I love you and I'm just keeping it real. I want you to understand what you're getting yourself into."

A smile comes over Maxine's face. "Ms. Che Che, I couldn't have said that any better myself. Thank you."

Trina finally decides to join the conversation but not until she lets out a nice loud belch. "Why can't we all just get along…just be happy for the girl? You all know she can blow. And plus, you never know what opportunities this could lead up to. This may open the door for her just like she said."

"I'm not here to rain on your parade Jada," Maxine said. "I'm simply suggesting that you wait for God's time. He'll provide an arena for your message if singing is what you want to do. He's the one who blessed you with that beautiful voice in the first place. So just believe that he'll provide you with the right stage for singing. You won't have to go to a club to sing just to get exposure and a little extra cash. I believe if you do this the way you're doin' it, it's like tryin' to serve two masters."

Trina jumps in. "We not in slavery days any more, Maxie. Whoever pays the big bucks is the Massah." She looks at Jada.

"So Jada, who's your Massah, I said who's your Massah?" Trina and Jada give each other a hi-five.

Ms. Che Che starts piling up the empty plates to take back to the kitchen. "What Maxine has tried to say to you is, if you're a Christian like you *proclaim* yourself to be, you shouldn't go anywhere or do anything that you can't include Jesus in. If Jesus came in the flesh, would you take Him to the club with you?"

"Of course not," Trina said. She pauses and thinks for a moment. "Wait a minute. Can Jesus juke? *Heyyyyy*!" Trina and Jada fall out laughing.

Maxine looks at them shaking her head. "Okay, you laughing now, but you sure won't be laughing while you jukin' in Hell. '*Heyyyyy*!'" Maxine mimics Trina's dance. "Just remember, my voice may very well be the last one you hear while you down there jukin'."

Ms. Che Che continues to pile the plates on the tray she brought for the dirty dishes. "Alright, I've heard and seen enough. I have plenty of hungry customers I need to tend to. Jada, just pray about it and hopefully you will make the right decision." She heads back to the kitchen.

Trina waits for Ms. Che Che to leave. "Maxie, what's all this jukin' in Hell stuff about? Don't you think you being a little bit too serious here? Just because you don't want to go clubbing and drinking doesn't mean everyone else has to stop!

Plus you done ran away Ms. Che Che! And you made me look bad."

"Yeah Maxie! You're being judgmental," Jada said.

"Don't misunderstand me. I'm not judging you; really I'm not! I love you guys. Pastor just spoke about the blessings and the curses that can come in your life based on what you do. Doesn't that scare you even a little to think that you can place a curse on your own life? He said that you're not really living unless you live for Christ."

Jada and Trina look at Maxine with such a blank expression.

Maxine throws her hands in the air. "That's it, I will say no more."

"No wait a minute, Maxie! I need you to understand that Pastor didn't mean it like that. He was talking about the sinners, he was talking about...," Jada pauses as if she's thinking about it and then yells "...*Trina*!"

This causes Maxine to burst out laughing with Jada... but not Trina.

Trina places her hand on her hip. "Don't be calling me a sinner."

"Well Trina, let's re-e-val-u-ate the si-chee-ation," Jada says. "*I'm* in the church, *I* was water baptized, and *I'm* filled with the Holy Spirit. *I* speak in tongues, *I* believe in Jesus Christ and His resurrection, *I* sing for the glory of God and *I'm* nice to all people. That means *I'm* bound for Heaven. *You* don't believe like *I* do so that would mean if Jesus came today, *you* would be in trouble my sister because *you…are… a… s-i-n-n-e-r.*"

Maxine shakes her head in disbelief.

"Wait just one minute, Miss Thang!' Trina said. *I* believe in Jesus and all that stuff you just said. *I* sit in church every Sunday just like you. I'm not involved in the church like you, but *I* believe. Even though I've never read the Bible for myself, doesn't mean *I* don't know anything. I believe Pastor's not gon' say anything up there that he shouldn't, so *I* trust him to tell me what the Bible's talking about. *I* too am a nice person. Matter of fact, I think I'm nicer than you. *You* just cursed out the man at the store this morning because he wouldn't give *you* change for a dollar to get on the bus to get to church."

"Now that's different. He had it coming. You don't see how he be actin' when I come in his little funky store. He's always lookin' at me like I stole somethin'. I don't appreciate that."

"You two like always, are missing the point," Maxine said. "It's not just about being nice and doing things in the church. Yeah it's good to be nice and to be involved, but your works here on earth isn't what gets you in Heaven. Your works is like your bonus for when you get to Heaven. This life is about the personal relationship you have with God. This walk with Christ isn't about you. It's about how *you* show *His* love. You have to show His love to other people and to Him as well. It's about *Him*, not *you*, *Him*."

"Okay Maxie, okay. You get so fired up at times. I'll tell you what; I'll make a promise. I promise I won't sing anything that's compromising to the faith." Jada takes Maxine's hand into both of her hands. "Don't worry girl, I'll never let anything persuade me or change me from being a Christian, I ain't crazy."

While Maxine approvingly nods at Jada's promise, Trina pulls her phone back out to see who else she can call. "Enough said. We need to go so we can get ready for tonight and get some good seats," Trina said. "Uhhh Jada, since you're the star, how about hooking a sister up with some tickets and a table up front?"

"Girl you know I got you. Plus you don't need a ticket to hear the band."

"Yeah, but you gotta pay to get in."

"I said I got you girl, now hush."

"I'm just checking."

"I said hush." Jada turns to Maxine. "Maxie, you in?"

"Nah, I'm going home. I got some things to do after the musical."

Trina moves over and gives Maxine a big hug. "Come on Maxie let's have some fun like the good old times. Just think, we'll also be supporting our girl here. Come on Maxie, please."

"Nah, you all just go ahead and get ready to have your fun. I'll be alright. Just call me when you ready to meet up for church." Jada and Trina grab their purses to leave. Maxine picks up her soft drink and begins to play with the ice in the glass. "I'll be praying for you, both of you."

"Now see, a lil' prayer ain't gon' hurt nobody," Trina said. "You do that and I'll call you later."

The girls stand and hug each other. Jada and Trina go to hug Ms. Che Che as she tries to act like she's more concerned with the volume of customers than the mindset of her favorite young ladies. Maxine sits back down while Jada and Trina leave.

Ms. Che Che looks over towards Maxine and decides to join her at the table bringing two nice big helpings of her delicious banana pudding. Maxine smiles at the sight of her favorite dessert.

Ms. Che Che sits down. "Can I say one thing Maxie?"
Maxine nods her head.

"I say this out of complete love for you." She pauses… "Don't be so heavenly bound, that you're no earthly good. You understand me?"

Maxine looks at her wondering what she really means. Ms. Che Che looks away and starts to eat as Maxine continues to think about her statement. Once Maxine realizes what Ms. Che Che is saying, she gives her a nod of understanding as they quietly eat their dessert.

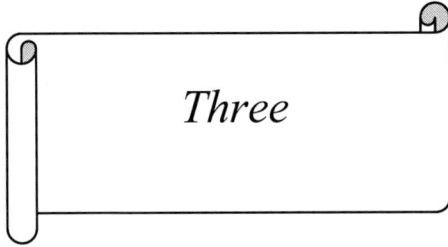

Three

*E*llie Addams clears the table from the dinner they picked up earlier at Che Che's Place as James sits there reading the newspaper. Ellie hadn't been in the mood for cooking. She was preoccupied and had been moping around the house since they made it home from church.

Ellie could still hear Pastor Devine's words echo in her head over and over again. *He said in His Word that He will make you the head and not the tail. I'm talking about a CEO, a president of a company! I'm talking about owner and operator of your own business. Can I get an Amen from somebody who wants to be the head, the leader, and not the tail, the follower?*

She's wondering why things can't be like that for them. When she married James Addams twenty-five years ago, things were so promising for them. He had a stable job with the airlines which was actually how they met.

She was on her way to see her grandmother in Atlanta. Her flight had been delayed and she went in one of the airport bars to watch TV and get a bite to eat. James was walking, pushing a luggage cart for a passenger when he first saw her. He thought she was the most gorgeous woman he had ever seen. He finished taking the passenger to her departure gate and came running back to the bar to talk to her. But when he returned, she was gone. He looked everywhere but couldn't find her. Just when he was about to give up, she walked up right behind him and asked if he could give her directions. They've been together ever since.

But where had they gone wrong…or had they gone wrong? What was holding them back…or were they held back? She pondered those thoughts as she looked over at James sitting at the table. Ellie picked up some bills that were scattered on the counter and started going through them.

"James, you see all these bills we got over here? When we gon' pay them? This one is thirty days past due. This one is three months past due. Look at this one; we haven't paid this one in over a year. And these charge cards; we've only been paying the minimum balance, and I swear every time I look at the new balance it hasn't changed one bit."

"Yeah Ellie I know," James says never looking up from the newspaper. "It looks rough right now but it's alright. Just pay the gas, electric, and definitely the cable bill. Forget that other crap. If it's already late, what difference will it make? They just gon' send another bill. So go ahead and throw those out. But don't worry, we're going to come into some money, I can just feel it. It may not be today, but one day. It might even be tomorrow."

"Look James. You've been telling me maybe not today, but tomorrow for twenty-five years. When is tomorrow gon' come?"

"Don't be looking down on me woman. I'm doing the best I can. You been moping since we came home from church. Now Pastor said some powerful things today, but you got to treat it like watermelon. You eat the part that's good to you and spit out the rest. You hear me?"

"Yes James, I hear you. But why do we have to be so behind all the time?"

"Look, things are not as bad as you see it right now. If we keep buying all those lottery tickets everyday, our numbers are bound to hit. I'm telling you, I can feel it."

"Then why don't we use some of the money we keep in the jar over there? You say it's for emergencies. Is paying bills an emergency? We only use the money for lottery tickets. And what about paying our tithes? I can't even remember the last time we paid tithes."

"Ellie, are you crazy? You must definitely be in a funk today because we've discussed this before. Let me explain it to you one more time. We pay tithes to ourselves by putting the money in the jar. The money in the jar is to play the lottery. That's our emergency fund and our emergency is to be rich and never have to work another day in our lives. Now listen Ellie, just stick to the game plan. You know what we trying to accomplish. Don't worry about church tithes. We pay an offering to the church from time to time. Once we hit big, then we'll pay tithes. You know Pastor Devine rather have it all in one lump sum anyway."

"You're probably right as usual. With us playing $25 daily for the morning, $25 for the evening lottery, and about $100 every week for the Big Money Lottery, our numbers are sure to come up. I'm sorry baby, I get so frustrated sometimes. That sermon kind of got me spooked."

"That's all right baby, I understand. But that's how we beat the system. We keep on playing all these numbers everyday, twice a day, our numbers will have to come up and then *bam baby— we millionaires*. Now just throw them bills in the garbage. We'll get to them; you know they gon' send them again."

LJ comes in the room looking down at his shoes. "Mom, I need some new shoes. These are falling apart."

James Jr., affectionately known as LJ, is Ellie's eight year old, little pride and joy, her miracle child. She had been very sick at age thirteen and the doctors performed a partial hysterectomy which was rarely done to a patient at that young age. Due to the surgery, she had been told that she could never have children. Ellie loved kids and this completely crushed her. Even James loved kids, but he told Ellie that it didn't matter. If God meant for them to have children, it would happen. And it did. Just when she thought her child bearing days were about over, it happened just like James said. Everything always happened as he said.

Now LJ was wise for his young tender age. He was high spirited and very inquisitive about everything in life. He took a particular interest in the stories his dad's sister would tell him from the Bible. Whenever anything was read to him, he would stare right at you the whole time and never move. Once you were through, he remembered every name and every event that occurred; and the things that would come out of this boy's mouth just amazed Ellie. His mind was a big sponge. He was a lot like his father, that's why his aunt nicknamed him LJ which stood for Little James. "Mom," he said again. "Look at my shoes. Dad told me he would get me some new shoes tomorrow. Well, today is tomorrow."

Ellie looked down at his shoes. "Yeah hon, they are looking pretty bad," she turns to her husband. "James, did you tell this boy you were gon' get him some shoes today?"

James doesn't even look up from the newspaper. "Nope!"

"James, you didn't say that?"

"Nope!"

She turns and faces LJ. "I just know you didn't come in here and tell your momma a lie just to get some shoes. I know you know better than that."

"Momma, I'm not lyin'. Daddy did say it."

LJ walks over to where his dad is sitting reading the newspaper. "Daddy, yesterday you said, 'I'm gon' get you some shoes on tomorrow'."

Ellie realizes what's going on, shaking her head laughing a little because she knows the reaction James will give LJ.

James responds, still without looking up. "What's today?"

"Sunday!"

"So *today* is Sunday."

"Yes sir it is."

"Did I tell you that I would buy you shoes on Sunday?"

LJ thinks about it for a minute. "No daddy, you didn't say Sunday, but yesterday you said you would buy my shoes tomorrow and today is tomorrow."

"I told you tomorrow. I never said I would buy your shoes today. I said tomorrow. Today is not tomorrow. Today is today and tomorrow is tomorrow, so like I said, I'll take care of it tomorrow. Now go on about your business."

LJ looks up at his dad in confusion. He puts his head down and slowly leaves the room.

"James, you shouldn't make promises you won't keep. You will break his lil' heart. And the boy really could use some shoes. Did you see the way they flappin' on the bottom?"

"I haven't broken any promises to the boy, Ellie. Now I said tomorrow so leave it alone. Now if you want to help, go get some string and tie it around the shoe until tomorrow." James laughs softly to himself. "I should've been a comedian."

The doorbell rings. Ellie goes to open the door without even asking who it is. James' sister, Peaches, comes over every Sunday after service like clockwork.

Peaches has the biggest smile on her face as Ellie opens the door. "Hey sis-in-law," Peaches says. "How are you? Y'all ran out of church so fast I didn't get to speak to you."

"Come on in Sis," Ellie waits for Peaches to come in and closes the door behind her. "What difference would it make if we ran out or stayed around? We know you gon' come by whether we see you or not."

"Yeah, but one day I'm gon' fool ya."

"Yeah right, not likely from where I see it," James yells from the kitchen. "I don't think we'll ever be that lucky."

"Oh, we got jokes today," Peaches said entering the kitchen. "Well, like I just said, how y'all doing?"

"I'm fine considering we broke. What about yourself?" Ellie asked.

"I'm so blessed by the best, what more can I say? But broke! Why you crying broke all the time? You got a job. Your big head husband over there got a job. What you doing with your money?"

Peaches walks over and hits James on the back. He looks up from the paper and gives her a nod and goes right back to reading. "Well I hope you paying your tithes 'cause God will bless your finances if you give back just a little bit of what He gives to you. But come on James, why Ellie on this 'we broke' kick again? Every time I come over here she talkin' about y'all broke."

James finally looks up from the newspaper. "Then maybe you should stop coming over!"

"Don't be silly. You not getting rid of me that easily. Plus, y'all ain't broke."

James puts the paper down. "We are broke! You know that we're saving our money to pay for that trip next year."

"James, you and Ellie have been saving for a trip as long as you two have been together and you still haven't gone anywhere. The thing that surprises me the most is that you work for the airlines, so we know you fly for free. You're always saying 'next year we going on a cruise', or 'we going sightseeing real soon'. I've come to believe that you afraid of flying." Peaches laughs and spots the money jar on the table. "Well, what about your so-called emergency money jar over there? That jar stays full of money so you must not have any emergencies. I should be asking you for some money."

"That's our investment jar," Ellie says. "We take money out of our pay checks every week and dump it in this jar so we can put it into our investments."

"Okay, investments, that's good. But Ellie, what kind of investments you making that you keep in a jar and keeps you crying broke all the time?"

"We've hit the lottery quite a few times, but not quite big enough yet. As long as we keep investing, we'll eventually win. You know what they say *"you gotta play to win"*.

James is shaking his head in agreement with Ellie as he continues reading his newspaper. "That's right Ellie, that's right."

At this time LJ walks in slowly with his head down still wearing his raggedy shoes. He sees his Auntie Peaches and his face lights up.

"Oh my goodness, look at my big boy. Come here LJ and give your auntie some love."

LJ almost does a flying leap into her arms. He gives Aunt Peaches a big hug as she kisses him on his forehead.

"Let me take a good look at my favorite nephew. Boy you're growing to be ..."

She takes a good look at him, puts him down and then turns him around towards his daddy. "James, have you seen this boy's shoes?" Peaches turns him around toward Ellie. "Ellie, look here, what's this? The sole of this boy's shoe is flapping back and forth. When you gon' get him some new shoes?"

James looks up from his paper. He looks at Peaches. He looks at LJ and goes back to the paper. "Tomorrow."

"James, the boy's shoes are talking to each other… *today*!"

"I said… *tomorrow*."

"Oh no, you won't use that on me James Eugene Addams! Remember I'm your sister. I know you and I don't want to hear about that tomorrow mess."

Peaches stoops down and holds LJ by the shoulders. "LJ, how long has your daddy been telling you tomorrow?"

"I don't know. Every time dad tells me tomorrow, tomorrow comes, but dad says tomorrow is not today, so tomorrow never seems to come. I get so confused, I don't know if today is today or if today is tomorrow or if tomorrow is yesterday. I guess I just have to wait until tomorrow comes. daddy will let me know when tomorrow comes."

"That's right boy, I'll let you know!" James holds the paper up to cover his face so that LJ can't see him laughing.

Peaches stands back up laughing with her hands on her hips. "Lord, have mercy on my family. You know LJ, your daddy been saying that for as long as I've known him. He thinks he's slick. He says that to get out of doing stuff. I'll tell you what, Auntie Peaches gon' buy you some shoes… *today*.

God blesses me real good and He just keeps on blessing me. So, Auntie Peaches gon' turn around and bless you right now. Now you go get ready."

LJ runs out of the room to get ready and Peaches yells to him, "And make sure you put on another pair of shoes. We'll leave those here so the dead can bury the dead."

James looks up from the paper, "you know you ain't funny."

"Now James, you know you wrong for mixing that child up like that. You're gon' confuse the boy so bad he's gon' end up in the nut house. Sometimes even Ellie sounds like she already rents a room up there. "

Peaches laughs at her own joke while Ellie frowns. James also laughs and Ellie quickly gives him a stern, unappreciative look. James clears his throat and puts the paper down. "Peaches, you need to stay out of our business when it comes to raising my boy."

"Well James, I'm concerned because we weren't raised like that. You go to church every single Sunday, you and your family. I don't think you've ever missed a Sunday since we were kids. Plus you the Head Deacon and all, so how you gon' act like that!"

"Oh shut up," he says grinning.

"How you got to be Head Deacon I'll never understand. I'm sure Pastor knows what he's doing."

"I hope he knew what he was doing when he made you Minister of Music. You never could sing!"

"Man I ain't thinking about you," Peaches laughs. "Don't you hear what Pastor Devine says up there in that pulpit?"

"I hear him and I hear him well. He talks real good too, but I ain't putting no money in Pastor's pocket 'cause he ain't put no money in mine. I know my job at the church and I do my job. I do it well. The church runs real good because of me. What I do here in my own house is my business."

"What you do here is God's business. You're a leader in the church so you must be an example to all others who are under your leadership or who just look up to you." Peaches glances back at the money jar. "Man, you broke all the time because you don't believe God is your source."

"Peaches, I know God is my source. That's why He's gon' help me win that lottery. When I win, I will be able to bless a many people, just like God wants it to be. Pastor says the Lord gives us ideas to obtain wealth in order to bless His people; so this is my idea from God."

"You honestly think God gon' help you win the lottery?"

"Yes I do. In due season."

"Don't you know who your source is?"

"Yes I do."

"Don't you know that if God is your *source*, He will give you your *resource*?"

"And that's exactly what the lottery will be, my *resource...*
from the source!"

"If you truly believed God was your source, you wouldn't
need to play the lottery. When you play the lottery you place
your trust in man and luck, not God. God wants you to look to
Him for all your wants and needs that He already has stored for
you! Your help will come from Him, not numbers."

Peaches walks over to the chair to sit down and pulls her
Bible out of her bag and holds it up in the air. "James, I know
this sounds crazy, but have you ever really read this?"

"Yeah, kind of! I know what I need to know in order to do
my hymn on Sunday morning." James clears his throat to give
Peaches a little of his deacon moan.

"Ummmmmm, I......, I, love the Lawd...awd ...awd,

Annnnnnnddddddd He heard my cry-eye-eye.......,"

Peaches looks at him like he's crazy. "You're kiddin',
right?"

"Nope, I'm not kiddin'! Don't act like you don't know.
And if you don't know you better ask somebody!"

Ellie is cracking up at the two of them.

"James, I don't know what to do with you. You should be
ashamed," Peaches says.

"Come on now Sis. Have you really noticed how many
pages in the Bible? It's like a big novel or something like that
book about that whale. And it's never ending!"

"Yeah and it says in the book of Psalms 119:11, *'Thy word have I hid in my heart that I might not sin against thee'*. You have to read the Word in order for it to get in your heart so that you can live the Word, James."

James balls his fist and shakes it at Peaches. "You just keep on talkin' Peaches. I'll hide something in your heart alright. I don't believe you up in my house quoting scriptures at me."

"Man, I'm not scared of you. You the one need to be scared. God wants you to read His Word for yourself so you will know what He wants from you. In this life you will have to take a test, so I suggest you read the Word so that you can pass the test."

Ellie walks over to Peaches. "Peaches, you shouldn't be coming over here throwing scriptures at us. We know what we doing. You may not understand it, but we do. Plus, Pastor already preached this morning, unless you come here to do the second half."

"Well said Ellie," commended James. "Sis, I must let you know that you're about to wear out your welcome! You cannot come in my house telling me what I should do."

"But James, I'm only—"

"Look Peaches and I mean this. I don't mind you getting LJ some shoes. That's your nephew and you should help out from time to time, but I do mind you coming in my house, contradicting me. I said one day and that's what I meant. One day I'm going to do a lot for my family. I'm gon' open up a landscaping business and buy a big house, with a big yard. I'm going to take them on vacations, buy Ellie and LJ all the clothes and anything else they could possibly want. When LJ is of age, I'm gon' get him a car, a fine car 'cause I already know he's gon' deserve it. One day, I'm going to do all that and more for my family...when I hit the lottery. You'll see. One day Peaches, I'm going to have it all; everything you could possibly imagine. But not this day, one day, just not today. My time has not come. I got plenty of time. So just go on about your business."

LJ comes into the room and Peaches leans down to hug him. She walks over to James and slightly kneels down to kiss him on his forehead. Peaches then moves over and hugs Ellie before leading LJ to the door. "I'm sure I will never be able to express how much I really love you two. You're the only family I have left besides my boys. I want you to just remember one thing and I say this out of complete love and respect for both of you. I've lost somebody near and dear to me and you all know what it did to me. Tomorrow is not promised. You said *one day*, but one day may never come. You need to make the most of *today, this day*. The Lord said, Give us This Day."

On that note Peaches takes LJ's hand and opens the door. Ellie walks behind them. Peaches turns around. "I'll drop LJ back off before I go to the church musical, or should I take him with me?"

James comes up to LJ. "You want to come back here or go to the musical?"

"I want to go to the musical. Sister Jada is singing with Auntie Peaches and they be jamming together."

"Your Auntie Peaches can't sing!"

"Dad!"

"Alright, alright little man. You can go. Plus your mom and I will be down to the church a lil' later. So we'll just pick you up there." He kneels down and gives LJ a big hug. "Don't wear your auntie out!"

"I won't dad. I love you."

"And I love you son." James stands and gives Peaches a long big hug. "Peaches, no matter what, I love you too."

Ellie ruffles LJ's hair and kisses him on the forehead before he heads out the door with his favorite Auntie Peaches.

Four

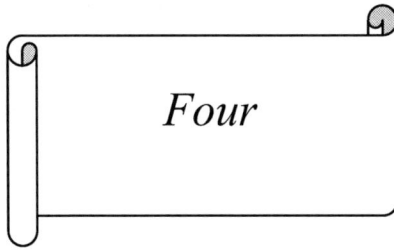

*I*t was jumping at the Holy Tabernacle Church's Annual Musical. Choirs from different churches and community groups were there getting their praise on. Joshua and Jacob Wright were hanging out in front of the church.

"Man, is it hot in there or what? And it's jam packed," Joshua said. "You want to run with me down to the store? I'm thirsty. My treat?"

"Naw man. We better stay here," Jacob said. "Mom would have a fit if she knew we left the church. They'll probably be through in about an hour, so we might as well just wait. You can treat then."

"She told *you* not to leave the church. She didn't say anything to me!"

"Well, then I guess that settles it. I'm staying here. I don't want to hear mom's mouth. You know how she can go off, especially when she catches us doing something she told us not to do!"

"Why you such a punk Jay? You scared she gon' take away your baby blanket or maybe even your Bible?"

"There you go, always trippin'. Just gon'!" Jacob says while laughing at his brother.

"Come on Jay. I don't want to go by myself. Plus if I went by myself and mom came out here and saw that you let me go by myself, you gon' be in trouble anyway. She's always telling us we have to stick together. So if you gon' get in trouble, you might as well get in trouble for something you did."

"You wrong for that man. I can't believe you."

"You know I'm right."

"Yeah, but you're the one who always get me in trouble." Jacob looks at his watch. "Let's just hurry up before mom gets through in there, and remember, you treatin'."

"I got you man. Now go put away your Bible."

"Naw man, dad got me this Bible. I can't just sit it down anywhere, someone may steal it."

"Put it up man 'til we come back."

"Look, if I go, the Bible comes with me."

"Fine. Let's go see what's goin' on inside first."

Joshua and Jacob go back into the church to take a quick peek before they leave and head to the store.

✤

Joshua and Jacob have always been tight especially since their dad died a few months back. It had been hard on their mom. She and their dad had a happy marriage and they all had a wonderful life together. They had their share of bad times but no matter what, they stuck together as a family. Jayden Wright had always preached that his boys were to stay together and stick up for each other no matter what happens, and their mom definitely reinforced everything Jayden said. That's why Jacob promised his dad, that he would look out for them, *no matter what*.

It was Jacob who found his father on the living room floor gasping for air. He didn't know what to do except call 911 while holding him in his lap. In the back of his mind, he wished Josh was there, he would know what to do. Josh always knew what to do and how to handle any situation. He loved his big brother and looked up to him. Normally Josh would've been home with him, but he had to stay after school for swim practice and Jacob did not feel up to hanging around the school, waiting for him.

They always walked home together after school or after Joshua's practice. Joshua was the athlete of the family and it was because of swimming that he had to learn CPR. Josh tried to get Jacob to learn as well. He would always say, "You never know when it may come in handy".

Well, the handy time had arrived and he couldn't do anything but hold his dad in his arms. Jayden made Jacob promise he would be the man he had been preparing him to be. Jacob kept telling him that he could never replace him and he was going to make it through for the sake of the family. Jacob kept telling his dad it was not his time yet, God was not ready for him because he still had work to do.

At first Jayden appeared to be struggling for air, but as Jacob talked to him, he seemed to have calmed down and appeared to be resting. When the paramedics arrived, they hooked him up to some strange equipment and moved with such urgency; but the expression on their faces told a grim story. They continued to work on his father even though they knew he could not be revived. Jacob always believed they did it for him. Jayden had actually died way before the paramedics had arrived. He died almost immediately after Jacob's vow, from complications due to asthma.

✠

As they were on their way to the store, talking and playing around with each other, they didn't notice the group of guys hanging out on the corner. One of the guys was sitting on the hood of an abandoned car. He jumped down as Joshua and Jacob were passing by.

"Hey man, where you church boys headin'?" asked Tiny noticing the Bible in Jacob's hand.

Joshua and Jacob continued on talking as they walked by Tiny, not hearing him. Tiny throws down his stuff and runs in front of Jacob and his boy Patch, runs behind Joshua. The brothers are startled.

"Hey man, I said where y'all headed? You just gon' ignore me like I ain't talkin' to you? You think you too good to talk to your friendly neighborhood thugs?" All the other guys start to laugh.

"Oh, I'm sorry man, we didn't hear you talkin' to us," Jacob said.

Tiny yells in Jacob's ear. "Well, can you hear me now? I said, can you hear me now?" Tiny knocks Jacob's Bible on the ground.

Joshua turns and faces Tiny. "Man what's up with you? We mindin' our own business, I suggest you mind yours."

"Oh we got a smart one right here and he thinks he's bad," Patch, one of Tiny's boys, said. "Let me bust his head for you Tiny. Right here and right now!"

Joshua raises his fist ready to take them all on. "Fool you ain't bustin' nobody's head today; especially not me or my brother."

Tiny taunts the brothers. "Oh man, my bad. That's your brother? I thought that was your woman." Everyone starts laughing.

Joshua starts to rush Tiny but Jacob grabs his brother to try to calm him down. Jacob tries hard to hold onto his brother. "Josh, it ain't worth it man. Let's just go. We don't need this."

Patch and some of the others start to circle around the brothers. "Well, well Tiny, I think this one is actually a lil' smarter than the other one."

"He may act smarter but he sho' don't look no smarter," Tiny says.

Joshua stands up to them. "We're way smarter than you or your boys will ever look."

Patch becomes real irritated with Joshua. "Just let me smash him one good time. I'll show him how to act around us. How to show us some respect!"

Joshua comes right back at him. "You ain't smashin' nothin' up in here. Jacob let me go. We not gon' let these punks just push us around."

Jacob is still trying to hold on to his brother. "It's not that important, let it go. It's just a misunderstanding. They thought we were dissin' them. It was an honest mistake. Let's just get back to the church before mom notices us gone."

"Oooh, we got us some momma's boys here. I bet y'all still on breast milk," yells out one of Tiny's boys.

Joshua once again tries to break loose from Jacob, but Jacob won't let go. "Josh, let it go man, please just let it go." Joshua finally pulls away from Jacob.

Tiny walks right up to Joshua and squares off pointing his finger in his face. "You better listen to your little woman over there, 'cause *she* just saved you, not your pathetic little god you left back at the church." He spits on the ground. "Maybe we'll just come and pay y'all a visit over there at that little church. Maybe you can save us too."

In an effort to keep the peace, Jacob pushes between Joshua and Tiny. "You and your friends will be more than welcome at the church."

Joshua is not buying Jacob's peacekeeping mission and squares back off with Tiny spitting on the ground. "Yeah, I got a special seat for all of y'all. By all means, bring it on."

"You still think you bad," Tiny said. "Well, this day just so happens to be your lucky day." Tiny turns from Joshua to look at Jacob. "I believe in giving women a chance. That was your chance, your only chance. If I ever catch you or that sissy over here again, we gon' have to show you how we treat people who disrespect us on our turf." Tiny opens his shirt to expose his gun. "Now little lady, take your man on home. I'm sure we'll meet again."

Jacob grabs Joshua by the arm. "Come on Josh. Let's get back to the church."

Joshua shakes loose from Jacob's grip. "We supposed to be going to the store. Remember, it's my treat."

"Forget the store man, let's go back to the church."

Patch is in the background mimicking the brothers. "Come on home honey, so we can talk about this over a nice cold bowl of Wheaties… or do you prefer Frosted Flakes?" All of Tiny's boys fall out laughing.

Joshua takes off down the street back to the church. Jacob picks up his Bible and runs trying to catch up with his brother.

"Wait Josh, wait!"

Joshua doesn't stop until they get back to church. Once Jacob finally catches up, Joshua immediately faces off with him. "I told you not to bring that Bible! And why you let them guys punk us?"

"Fist for fist is not always the answer to everything. You can't beat everybody down, Josh. Sometimes we have to learn to turn away anger with a soft answer."

"Soft answer my behind. What's wrong with you man! What you did was make them guys think *we were soft*! Now they gon' always step to us."

"This is one of those situations where we just need to pray about it. We can't sit back and worry about what they gon' do or when we gon' run into them again. We can just go pray about it and let it go. Fighting is not always the answer Josh. Think about what dad would've done!"

"You know what Jacob, you're starting to sound just like yo' momma. I believe dad would've whipped every one of those fools right there on the spot."

"Well if you think that, then think about what would Jesus have done?

"Jesus would've called on His league of angels and messed all them punks up!"

"I should've known you would say something like that. But you know what, the part about mom, I consider that a compliment."

"Jay, you're scaring me boy." Joshua heads towards the door of the church.

Jacob grabs his arm again and turns him face to face. "Look Josh, we didn't have any business leaving the church in the first place. This is the kind of thing that always happens when we're hard-headed."

"Momma better get married again and put a male figure around you quick, fast and in a hurry. I swear to God if you turn soft on me I will beat you down and those same punks will be the ones that will have to pull me off you."

"Josh, don't swear to God, and why I gotta be soft just because I think about the best way to handle a situation before I act on it? Mom keeps telling us to fight with our mind not our fists. She says to take it to God first so He can handle it."

"Jay, sometimes we can't be waiting on God to step in. He helps those who help themselves. What happens if someone pulls out a gun? You saw he was packing! What you gon' do, kneel down and pray?"

"That's not a bad idea."

"I didn't mean that literally man. By the time God sends help all the way down from Heaven, it could be too late for us. We need to handle our business and let God pick up the pieces."

"I don't want Him picking up the pieces. I want God in on it from the beginning."

Joshua looks at Jacob conspicuously. "You gon' be a preacher or somethin'?"

"Naw man, I ain't no preacher. I just believe God's Word."

Joshua continues to look at Jacob. "You sure you ain't gon' be no preacher?"

Jacob pauses and thinks about it again. "Not unless you gon' be my Armor Bearer, that's probably the only job in the church I think you qualify for."

"Yeah," Josh says rubbing his chin. "I think I would like that. Somebody got to watch out for you, and I do believe I'm the person for the job."

"Okay man, you're hired, now let's get inside before mom catches us. And believe me, them goons ain't got nothing on momma."

The boys go back inside the church never telling anyone about what happened.

One Day…This Day!

Five

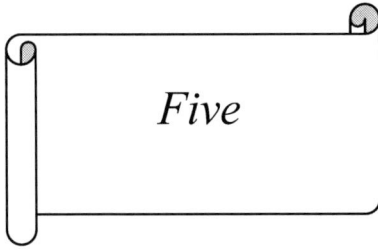

*I*t was a packed house and the deejay was slamming. The Wild Card had never been this crowded. The word had gotten out about the new live band Eklyptic making its debut appearance and anyone who knew anything about clubbing was not willing to miss this live performance. The deejay knew the mass crowd was there for the live band, so he wanted to make sure he put it down so hard, that they wouldn't forget how good the dance music was. Almost everyone was on the dance floor doing it up real hard.

It was time for the deejay to slow it down and allow the people to get to their tables before the start of the performance. They hadn't realized that while they were dancing, the band had already moved to their places. The lights were turned up but not too bright. The band chimed in immediately as the deejay faded his music out. People rushed to get their drinks so they could have what they needed while the band played.

This move was completely new for the Wild Card and its manager, Ramón Thompson. He wanted everything to be perfect. Eklyptic, which was a full fledge band with horns, strings, keyboards and a drummer, was hired on a trial basis for the club. Ramón wanted to do something really different to bring more people in. And he had placed a big gamble on this live band idea. He and his business partners fronted big money for this gig and now it was time for the big pay off.

The lights changed from being slightly dim to a sparkling display of different colored lights fading in and out. While the band softly played, Ramón stepped onto the stage introducing each member of the band as they played brief solo pieces. The crowd excitedly clapped at just the newness of it all. Then he introduced the new singing sensation.

Trina's tables went wild with excitement as Jada strolled onto stage. Her presence had a way of demanding attention and every eye in the house was on her. She was elegantly dressed in a white and silver sequin mid-length dress, with matching white and silver pumps. The dress accented her shapely figure; it didn't hide a lot, but it hid just enough. All her seductive body parts were well emphasized. Her hair was swooped into a pin-up with a matching silver comb and of course, matching silver earrings. She looked like a goddess; she looked perfect. But that was only the beginning of something beautiful.

As Ramón introduced her, she didn't come in and do a play with words talking about how she got to this moment, or the band's history or even a prelude to the song. Jada just strolled in and opened her mouth and sang. The entire audience was completely mesmerized. She was perfectly pitched, perfectly poised, perfectly groomed—just perfectly perfect.

Not a sound was heard in the club while she sang. Not only was the audience awestruck at the melodious sounds from this new singer, but the band as well as Ramón and his business partners seemed to be caught up in her passionate vocal ability. All while she sang, he and his partners nodded their heads, thoroughly captivated. When Jada sang, she had a way of taking complete control of her surroundings.

Trina sat there overwhelmed with tears flowing down her face. She kept dabbing at them quickly 'cause she didn't want anyone to see her like that. She wasn't a punk and she definitely wasn't the emotional type so she had to be cool. It was just so hard because she was so proud of her friend. And more importantly she was sitting at the VIP table with her boyfriend Mychal, the love of her life. She never wanted him to see her cry. He might think she was soft and try to take advantage of her and she was not having that!

Jada must've sung about four songs and the applause after each one was thunderous. People were amazed at her voice. Some were under the impression that she was an established artist they couldn't quite remember. When she ended her last song and thanked the crowd, the place went crazy. First there was the applause, and then the standing ovation as Jada took her bows. Not only did all the people in the audience stand, but the band stood as well, almost as if they had never heard her before this day. Tears welled up in Jada's eyes.

The ovation lasted a good five minutes, or so it seemed. They even started a chant, "More Jada! More Jada! More Jada! More Jada!". Ramón immediately got up on stage and took the microphone. He didn't want a riot and people seemed to be that pumped up. "Everyone, please give it up for the fabulous Jada Jenkins and the Eklyptics." The people continued to clap and chant. He turned his attention to Jada. "Miss Jenkins, we know you were only supposed to do a few numbers, but could you please do one more song before we have a riot up in here!" At that, the audience once again gave a thunderous applause as they whistled, yelled and screamed her name.

Jada smiled and walked over to the band director and whispered something in his ear. He immediately cued the musicians as they began to play once again. The audience went crazy again as Ramón walked off the stage to let Jada do her thing. This time she began to talk to her audience. "You know, I can get used to this. I wasn't sure if we were going to be able to come back and do this again, but what you think? You think you might want us to come back and entertain you again?"

The crowd responds passionately to her questions. She smiles and looks at the band. They are playing softly, waiting for her cue. Now this excites her immensely. They are waiting for her, her cue…not her waiting for someone else's cue. Has she finally arrived? On that thought, Jada gives it all she has to give. Together, Jada and the Eklyptics wow the audience. As she sings, she even moves down from the stage into the audience. She has completely won over every heart in the club.

Jada finally ends the song, takes her bows and makes her way to the VIP tables where Trina stands there frantically clapping and crying. The ovation continues even after she makes it to the table. She turns to the crowd, takes another bow and motions to the audience to take their seats as the band ends the music. Another hot second later, the deejay went right back to spinning out a popular dance song while the people returned to the dance floor.

Trina managed to wipe that final tear she didn't want anyone to see, but it was pretty obvious she had been crying. She clapped so excitedly that her hands hurt. Once Jada was close enough to her, she grabbed her and they just hugged. "Girl I'm so proud of you. That was the bomb! You ain't never sang that good in church. Maybe this is your thing after all, just like you said."

Jada was tickled pink and smiling as wide as she could. "That was good wasn't it? It just felt so right, Trina. I could do this every night."

Mychal stood beside Jada and gave her a big bear hug, raising her up in the air. "Mychal! Boy, put me down. I don't know who's the craziest, you or Trina. You two are perfect for each other."

Mychal puts her down. "Your highness, may I pull out your chair? Your throne awaits you," He bows down before her while Jada looks at him like he's crazy. He stands up and lets the chair out so that Jada can take her seat. He does the same for Trina. The girls continue to hug while sitting at the tables. Mychal goes around to his seat and pours champagne in the fancy flutes provided by the Wild Card.

Mychal hands them their champagne glasses. "A toast to the most talented singer on this side of Heaven. Jada, in the famous words of your girl Trina, *you're the bomb*. I mean that was some sho-nuff straight-up sangin'!" They all clink their glasses in celebration. Mychal and Trina drain their glasses and pour another round. "Did you hear the way they were clapping for you?"

"No Mychal, she's deaf in one ear and blind in the other," Trina said this like Mychal's question was absolutely ridiculous. "Of course she heard the clapping. I think the loudest clapping came from this section right here!"

Mychal and Trina empty their glasses again and pour another round. Jada places her glass down on the table without drinking any. "Yeah I heard all that and I definitely heard your big mouth, I should say, big mouths. But can you believe it? This was amazing! I wish Maxie could've been here to share this with us."

Ramón and his business partners walk over to the table where Jada and her friends are sitting. "I see you have already started the celebration."

"Well, yes we have and I must say thank you. Mychal told me you provided us with the champagne," Jada said. "I appreciate that."

"You're more than welcome. You cannot know how much we appreciate you. But if you don't mind, I would like to take just a moment of your time to introduce you to several of the people responsible for you and the band's appearance. They are very eager to meet you and very happy with their investment."

Ramón introduces his partners, Dominique Newsome, Symone Crystals, and Arnell Jones, to Jada, Trina and Mychal. Mychal stands and shakes their hands while Jada and Trina remain seated and nod.

"Well," Ramón said, "we don't want to intrude on or delay your celebration even further. We just wanted you to know that we enjoyed you, and anything you want and I do mean anything, please…just let us know. You definitely have a future here at the Wild Card and in the music business."

"Not only do you have a future in the music business," Dominique Newsome said, "I'm here to assist you in making that transition." He hands Jada his business card. "Think about it and give me a call. If I don't hear from you soon, I'll find you."

Trina snatches the card. "Oh don't you worry. My girl gon' call you and if she doesn't, I will. Matter of fact, I'm her business manager or agent or whatever you call it. So from here on, all calls will come through me."

Jada smiles at Trina, stands up and extends her hand to them as they are about to depart. "Once again, thank you very much. I'll…" she looks over at Trina, "we'll be in touch." The business partners head back to their table.

"Wow Ms. Thang," Mychal says. "You work fast. This is your first night and they all over you like that! But it's not like you don't deserve it. Jada you really were good out there."

Out of excitement, Jada takes big gulps of her champagne, drinking it all. She notices another person approaching the table.

"Excuse me, I know you're busy and I don't mean to interrupt your party. I just wanted to tell you how talented you are and how much I enjoyed you tonight. I must say you completely blew me away. It's like I've heard that sound before. Matter of fact you look familiar too, but I just can't place it."

Trina jumps in. "Yes you did mean to interrupt and you need to come with a better line than that. Just keep it real my brother! Keep it real. If you have any business cards, talk to me."

Jada kicks Trina under the table. She places her empty flute down and motions Mychal to fill it again. "Well thank you sir, I appreciate the compliment."

"Please, please, not the sir thing. My name is Aaron Watson. Can I offer you a drink?" He extends his hand.

Jada holds up her flute and does not extend her hand to his.

Aaron pulls back. "I'm sorry, that was stupid. I was so taken by your performance I can't get my thoughts right. Well it's obvious that you're celebrating here and I'm interrupting. Once again, I apologize."

Jada realizes her rudeness and smiles at him. "Once again, I thank you but there's no need for your apologies. Your kind words are appreciated. If any apology is needed, it should come from us. I apologize for my ghetto girl here and for me not taking your hand. This has been such an amazing night but no excuse for our rudeness." She's also thinking— *now this is what I call eye candy!*

Aaron smiles and extends his hand again.

She shakes his hand. "I'm Jada Jenkins and this is my girl Trina Hendricks and her boyfriend Mychal… Wait a minute, Mychal, you got a last name? I can never remember it!"

"Willoughby."

"Willoughby? No wonder I keep forgetting," they all laugh.

Aaron shakes everyone's hand. "Nice to meet you all!"

Mychal chimes in. "Come on Aaron, have a seat. I could use some more testosterone over here."

Trina shouts out, "How much money you packin'?" Mychal pops her on the shoulder.

"Okay Trina, mind your manners!" Jada says as she quickly drinks more champagne. "Please Aaron, I agree with Mychal. Please sit down and join us."

As Aaron pulls out a chair, Mychal turns toward Trina. "That's rude! I know you ain't shallow like that. How you gon' ask a brother about his pockets? That ain't cool Trina."

"As good as Jada sounds and look, we got to protect her and be sure of the company she keeps. It's a lot of predators and straight up crazy people out here."

Aaron sits next to Jada and takes her hand and looks directly in her eyes, yet talking to Trina. "Well I guess I can understand you trying to protect someone so exquisite— and no disrespect to you Trina of course, but Jada is quite a beautiful and talented lady. And I'm sure she's old enough to make adult decisions about the company she wants to keep."

"Touché my brother," Mychal said.

"Oooh," Trina said, "maybe I was wrong about this brother. I hope your wallet is as sweet as your lines."

"Well," Aaron said, "let's just say I have enough for whatever you young ladies desire." He pulls out a hundred dollar bill and throws it down on the table. "Drinks are on me!"

Mychal sits up straight and rubs his hands together. "My man, you need to hang with us more often. Uh, you did include me in with this, right?"

Aaron nods at him. "Help yourself Mychal."

"Now you done messed up," Trina said. "How you gon' come over here flexing your wallet muscles like you got it like that? You perpetratin'! We already got free champagne and you know it. That's the only reason you came over here flashing your money around. Man I know your type."

"Trina, you've grossly misjudged me and somehow we've gotten off on a bad note and for that I apo—"

"There he goes again with another lame apology." She looks over at Jada. "See, I was right in the beginning. You stick around him and you gon' be sounding just like him, lame!"

Mychal puts his hand over Trina's mouth. "Aaron, I'm so sorry about my woman here, she's had a whole lot of champagne, she's excited about tonight, and she's very protective about her girl, Jada here. In actuality, she really is a sweetheart as you saw for a very brief moment." He removes his hand and kisses her on the lips. "But anyway, she's my lil' sweetheart." Trina responds to his kisses and snuggles closer to him. It seemed to calm her down some.

Jada drinks the rest of her champagne. "Aaron, please don't pay her any attention. Believe me, nobody else does." Mychal laughs while Trina just snuggles even closer to him. "But unfortunately, I have to turn down your offer. I believe I've already had more than enough to drink, plus I'm tired." Jada puts her empty glass on the table.

Mychal looks at her in surprise. "Come on Jada. The night is still young and I like this brother. Not yet! One more round."

All Trina could say was, "Yeah."

Jada stretched out her arms into the biggest yawn. "I'm good for the night. It's been a long day for me. I sang at the morning service, the afternoon musical and now here. Plus this champagne is making me light headed. I'm turning in."

Trina pulls away from Mychal. "Jada, you must be crazy. This man is giving us money. I'm not trying to like him but I guess he's okay. The people here are lovin' you and you want to go home? I feel the spirit of Maxie hovering around this table." She raises her hands in the air and waves her fingers as if spirits are all around them.

"Trina stop trippin'," Jada said. "Look Aaron, It was wonderful meeting you. I appreciate your generosity, but I'm just tired, nothing personal. Let's go my people."

Aaron snaps his finger. "Wait a minute. I knew your voice and face was familiar. That was you at Holy Tabernacle Church Annual Musical."

Jada looks surprised. "Yeah, that was me. You were there? What you doing going to a church musical?"

Aaron was surprised at her response. "You know, I could ask you same thing."

"No you can't" Jada said. "This is different, I'm working."

"For who?" Aaron asks.

"Oooh, this guy is good," Mychal said. "Man I like you more and more!" Mychal pulls at his collar. "It's burning up in here." Mychal is starting to feel the effects of the alcohol.

"Oh no, Maxie done sent one of her spying angels," Trina said as she snaps her fingers.

"Who is Maxie?" Aaron said.

"Don't play! We know who sent you. I knew this was a set up. I knew it when you first walked up. Where she at!" Trina stands up looking around for Maxine. "Where she at? Where is she? I know she's here hiding out! Miss Holy Holy couldn't resist it."

Mychal pulls Trina back down. "There you go again. It's definitely time to take you home."

"Trina," Aaron said. "I assure you I was not sent here by anyone. A friend of mine goes to that church and invited me to the musical." He looks at Jada. "Wow! Actually I can't say which one I enjoyed the most! You're definitely quite the talent."

Jada pushes her chair back and Aaron jumps up to assist her. "Well thanks a lot, but I must be going. Thanks for your kindness. It was a pleasure meeting you Aaron"

"I hope to see you again Jada. Is this here your thing or is the church more of your venue?" He pulls his card out of his jacket pocket and hands it to her.

"Well since you already know two of my hangouts, pick the one that's comfortable for you." Jada extends one hand to Aaron and then takes the card with the other.

He kisses her hand. "Let me walk you to your car."

"Actually I'm not driving. Mychal and Trina will be dropping me off if I can pull those two apart. But as for now, I will excuse myself to the little girls' room." She looks at Mychal and Trina. "You guys better be ready by the time I get back." Mychal nods to confirm Jada's request as she leaves the table.

Aaron stands there and watches Jada until he has lost sight of her in the crowd. He turns to Trina and Mychal. "She's something else. Uhhh, Mychal, can I speak to you for a quick moment?"

Mychal sits up. "Yeah man, no problem." He kisses Trina on her head and gets up from the table and staggers a little over to where Aaron is standing.

"I just want to put something in your head," Aaron whispered. "There has been some heavy drinking going on here and I'm not saying you can't handle it, but I would be more than happy to take all of you home…if that's alright with you. Maybe you can call me in the morning and we can come back and pick up your car. I mean, whatever you think is best."

"You know what man… that's awfully nice of you. And I'm not that shallow where I…, where I…." Mychal scratches his head while trying to remember what he wants to say. "Oh yeah…," he continues. "Where I would be *intimi…*, *intimi….* *Inti-mi-dated* by your offer."

Aaron quietly laughs as Mychal tries to speak. "You gon' be alright, man?"

Mychal glances over at Trina, holding on to Aaron's shoulder for balance. "We will… take you up on that. I'll make arran…, arran—"

"You'll make arrangements for the car in the morning?"

"Yeah, that's what I'm saying. Thanks. Good looking out!"

"No problem, but I can't say it's not a little selfish on my part. It gives me just a little more time with Jada."

"Okay, just let me tell the girls. They ain't gon' like it, but I can handle them."

"Good, I'll just go pull up the car. I'll be in the white Maxima. Can you make it alright?"

"Yeah man, give me a moment. I think I jumped up too fast."

Mychal sits down at the table and talks to Trina. She notices too that Mychal might not be able to drive and nods to Aaron. Aaron leaves to get the car.

Trina watches Aaron leave as Mychal tries to clear his head. "You know he's kind of cute and might be good for Jada. Lord knows she could use a good man and some good sex, so she won't be so uptight all the time like Maxie. It's been so long since she had a man, she might not even know what to do with one. But no matter how cute he is, there ain't nobody as fine as you baby."

Mychal throws a little water on his face from the water goblet on the table. "You know, I think he would be perfect for her, and we just met him. Somethin' 'bout that brother tells me, he's *genu…, genu—*"

"Genuine?"

"Yeah that's it. I guess I have had one too many. Mychal leans over and kisses Trina over and over again not seeing that Jada has returned and has sat down at the table, watching their lovesick antics.

Jada adds, "Yeah, you are drunk. And yeah, he seems genuine, but the man ain't saved. I have told you over and over that my man must be saved."

Startled at Jada's quick return, Trina and Mychal start gathering up their things to leave. Mychal stops to think for a minute, "Wait a minute, saved like you?"

"Yes, like me."

He places his coat back down. "Jada, don't start ragging on the brother and judging him," Mychal said. "How you know he ain't saved?"

"Well—"

"He said he was at your church musical today! So what does that say?"

"But—"

"But nothing! You don't know anything about him—and you know what, I think you've just cleared my head up with that remark. So let me say this before I start sounding like a babbling idiot again."

"Wait, Mychal, its not that serious."

"Let me say this. I've always wanted to say this and this situ...ation has just opened the door. I can't tell Christians apart from anybody else, 'cept for that Maxine and I think she's too radi..., radi—"

"Radical," Trina finishes.

"Yeah, thanks baby. Radical! But you know what, she actually might be on to something. Most folks I see in the church... I see at the clubs... I see on the boat... I see standing in them long lottery lines, smoking cigarettes outside the church, getting drunk, living together, you name it."

"That's right. It can be confusing and I never thought of it that way. Shoot, I guess if you look at it like that, you could be talking about me! So you know what baby…you speaking the truth," Trina said.

Mychal smiles at Trina, "I am, ain't I?"

"Yes baby, you are?"

"So," Mychal continues, "the million dollar question is this. If I can't tell 'em apart, how you gon' tell 'em apart? Where's the line actually drawn?"

"Ain't nothing wrong with all of that, with the exception of the fact that you're drunk, Mychal," Jada says. "The Bible doesn't say anything against smoking, gambling, dancing or partying and I've read it backwards and forwards. The Bible talks about you, and the state you're in right now, but that other stuff is fine. As long as I do what I'm supposed to do on Sunday and continue to pray and read my Word, I'm living the life of a Christian. God gave me a gift and as long as I'm using it for His glory He's fine with that! I don't murder, steal, cheat or lie or at least I don't think I lie. So if you want to know where the line is drawn, just look at me! Now let's go…*heathens.*"

Six

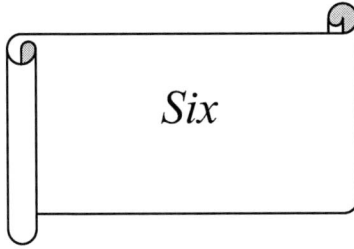

*L*ife became pretty hectic for Jada since that first night at the Wild Card. Her weeks became consumed with rehearsals and gigs, since accepting the contract to perform every Thursday through Saturday night with Eklyptic. She made sure no dates of her night club performances would interfere with any of her church rehearsals or performances. She wanted everyone to know that the church work was more important than anything else and it had to come first.

This schedule left her with Sunday through Wednesday to relax from the club even though she also had to find time for the band. Jada decided that the best day to rehearse with the band would be Tuesday and Wednesday, just before the performances. This would leave her with Monday as her only off day since she sang in the choir on Sundays, which was actually perfect. Monday would be her one day to wind down and rest from the club and church. It was very rare for something to be scheduled at church on this day.

Choir rehearsal was every Thursday at 6:00 p.m. and it usually lasted a couple of hours. This was one of those rehearsals where Jada was real tired and caught herself falling asleep a few times. Actually this was starting to happen a lot. She got up to go get some fresh air.

As Jada was heading out of the sanctuary, she overheard an argument escalating in one of the meeting rooms. Jada stood there for a moment to hear what was being said. She recognized Joshua and Jacob's voices and could tell Joshua was real upset. Jacob was trying to convince Joshua that they should tell someone what had been happening between them and some local boys. Josh on the other hand felt as though they did not need to tell and they would not have had any problems if Jacob hadn't wimped out on them earlier. Jada felt that this was pretty serious and was about to enter the room when Joshua rushed out almost knocking her down.

"Hey! I am so sorry Sister Jada. I didn't see you coming," Joshua said.

"That's okay Joshua, but slow down. What's going on in here? I could hear you two all the way in the sanctuary."

"We're sorry, it's not that serious," Joshua continues.

"Are you sure? It sounded pretty serious to me. I think we should talk, I got some time before I have to sing again."

"I'm telling you Sister Jada, everything is *copasetic*. Plus I gotta run, my mom called me into the sanctuary."

Jada looks at him puzzled. "*Copasetic?* What is—" Joshua takes off leaving Jada and Jacob in the halls. "Wait Josh!" She calls for Josh but he does not look back and enters into the sanctuary. Jada looks at Jacob. "You gon' tell me what's going on? And what is '*copasetic?*"

"Copasetic? That's just Josh's word for okay. And what you heard…it's nothing…well it's something, but Josh doesn't think it's major."

"Well, what do you think? Is it major to you? You know you can talk to me Jay."

"I know Sister Jada, but the more I think about it the more I agree with Josh. Plus I am praying about it."

"Jay, I heard what you all were talking about, and I think you need to tell someone, at least tell Pastor if you don't want to alarm your mother. You two are like my little brothers and I care about what happens in your lives. I know what you all have been going through in the past few months since—"

"Sister Jada, I know you don't mean no harm and I don't mean to cut you off or any disrespect, but we got this, really we do. If you really want to help, just pray for us. Pray that the Lord will lead us and guide our family in the way that we should go. Could you do that for me? Could you do that for us?"

"Of course Jay, I—"

"Thanks Sister Jada, I gotta go." Jacob hugs Jada and goes into the sanctuary behind Joshua.

"Wow, that did not go too well," Jada says out loud. She remembers that she was on her way out to get some air when she sees the members leaving out of the sanctuary indicating that rehearsal has just let out. "Ooh, I didn't know it was that late. This is perfect timing," she says again out loud. Jada looks down at her watch realizing that it's time for Trina to pick her up.

Her gig tonight at the Wild Card was at 9:30 p.m.. and she wanted to get to the club to relax a little before the show. She felt her voice struggling a little earlier during choir rehearsal so she pulled back somewhat and didn't sing as strong as usual. She needed to make sure her voice would be ready for tonight as well as the next few days. She wondered if all this singing, six days a week, would take a toll on her throat and her voice, as she headed out the church to look for Trina.

Jada is standing at the curb looking down the street, when Maxine spots her. "Come on Angel, I'll introduce you before she gets away. Maxine and Angel walk up to Jada. "Jada, I was looking all over for you. I want to introduce you to our new choir member. You came in a little late today and missed the introductions. You also left out early too. So Angel, this is

Jada Jenkins one of our anointed lead singers. Jada, this is Angel Buchanan."

"Nice to meet you Angel. Welcome to the choir. I'm sorry I didn't come to introduce myself earlier, but I had some things to do."

"Oh, that's quite alright," Angel said. "I'm happy to meet you finally. I must agree, you truly have a beautiful voice. God has really anointed you."

Jada was not really paying attention to Angel. "Yeah, I know. He has blessed me." Jada continues to look up and down the street for Trina.

"So Ms. Blessed by the Best, what you doing tonight and who you looking for?" Maxine asks.

"I'm waiting for Trina."

"Not that lil' roughneck," Maxine laughs. "Where y'all heading?"

"She's going with me to the Wild Card."

"Jada, we just got out of choir rehearsal!"

"Don't start on me Maxie. Now tell me…and I know you know! But what do you really think I've been doing these past few weeks?"

"Honestly, I don't know. And I think I'm afraid to ask."

"I never came right out and said anything 'cause… you never asked, even though I felt you knew. Well, just for the record, I perform Thursday through Saturday at the Wild Card.

The pay is real good. If you were a friend, you would come and hear me sing."

"I didn't know our friendship was based on me coming to the club to hear you sing, when I can hear you sing at church. And I didn't know you were hanging out there, especially since we never talked about it again. I guess that was just wishful thinking on my part. But Jada, tell me that you understand that something is wrong with that picture."

"I knew I shouldn't have said anything to you. I should've left well enough alone!"

"Angel, I need to talk with Jada, I'll catch up with you later."

"No problem Maxie," Angel replied. She looks over to Jada and holds out her hand. "Once again, nice to meet you Jada." Jada continues to look down the street for Trina, completely ignoring her. Angel looks at Maxine then turns and leaves.

Maxine can't believe what she just witnessed from her best friend. She knew she had been acting different lately, especially since her schedule had become so hectic and they no longer met at Ms. Che Che's during the week. But it was not like her to be straight up rude. Not like that!

"Look Jada, I'm your friend, your best friend. You've been my girl since we were five years old. We've always been as thick as thieves. What's going on with you? Why you acting like that?"

"If we were as thick as thieves, why you bringin' this girl all up in my face?"

"Don't try to change the subject on me and you need to stop trippin'. You were pretty dog gone rude to her."

"I don't care nothin' about her. I just want to know why you trippin' on me." She stops looking down the street for Trina and turns toward Maxine. "Maxie, we haven't really hung out in weeks and I would like for you to come see me perform. It would mean so much to me. All of our friends have come, even some from the church. If they can come, you can come!"

"Of course Jada, we can hang out, but not like that. Oooh... so that's what all this attitude is about. It also explains why some of the choir members act strange when I mention you. That's what they trying to hide. Well...I'm sorry. I can't do that, I can't come. The club is not the place for a Christian."

"What's that suppose to mean? I'm a Christian."

"You're right, you are and I'm sorry. I didn't mean it like that and I'm not placing judgment or doubt on your faith. I'm just concerned about everything that's going on with you."

"You sure don't act like it."

"You can't seem to understand the type of love I have for you. You can't even understand the love I have for God. I cannot sacrifice the things I strongly believe in just to satisfy you Jada. I cannot even believe that you would want me to."

"How can you say that? You know how important this is to me. It's not always about you Maxie. You have to think about others from time to time."

"Now that's a news flash. I cannot believe those words came out of that mouth. In our entire friendship, it has never been about me. I've catered to you all of our lives. But once I developed my relationship with God, I learned to put things in my life in its proper place. I love you…and I love God. But let me tell you something, Jada, I love God more than I love myself. That's how I keep myself in check. Ms. Che Che told me in so many words that I cannot be so Heavenly bound or holy holy as Trina puts it all the time. I need to balance it out so that I can actually reach people and not make them pull away. So I've pulled back, but one thing won't change Jada. God will always come first."

"I know we're supposed to love God and put Him first, but He tells us the most important thing is that we love each other."

"That's right, but He didn't say we were to love each other or even *ourselves* more than we love Him."

"Whatever, Maxie! I don't know who you think you're fooling!"

"Who I'm fooling! Who do you think you fooling?" Maxine starts to pace and then stops. "You know those songs you sing are so beautiful and you sing with so much conviction, people would swear you believed them or even lived them."

"What's that supposed to mean? Now you trying to look down on me Maxie? Is that what you call yourself doing? Well let me tell you something! I do believe and live the songs I sing, but you take it to the extreme. It does not take all that to be saved! You need a man, that's what's wrong with you. That was my problem too so it ain't like I don't understand."

"Girl please! I'm not about to go there with you. You cannot continue to live like this and call yourself a Christian. You have to make this thing personal. You need to choose! You need to stop this before its too late and stop focusing on the things of this world, like you and that club. You need to focus on God and only God. I would really hate to go to Heaven and not find you there." Maxine pauses, "And what do you mean not having a man *was* your problem?"

By this time, Trina has pulled up next to them but they're so into their argument that they don't hear her blow the horn. Trina gets out of the car and walks up totally unnoticed by either of them.

Jada ignores Maxine's last remark. She knows Maxine must've known something was going on with her and Aaron, especially since Aaron has visited a few times on Sunday. He even went to Ms. Che Che's with them afterwards. "There you go again like you the only one going to Heaven. Tell me right now what I do that's so bad that I won't get in but you will of course."

Trina steps right in between them. "Uh-oh! What did I just walk into?"

"It's about time you got here," Jada yells at Trina. "Since you're here…*late*, let me tell you what's going on with Miss *Holy-Holy-Never-Sin-Bound-For-Glory.* She's going to tell us why we're *going to Hell*."

"What you mean…*we*? Trina asked. "I just got here!"

"Trina, just hush while Miss Heavenly Bound tells us about our destination to Hell!"

Trina smiles. "Look, Maxie don't need to tell me nothing. I know I'm going to Hell, especially with what me and Mychal did last night. Oooh, baby!" Trina starts to do her signature dance.

Jada and Maxine ignore Trina. Trina stops dancing when she notices they aren't laughing at her as usual. She realizes that this is more serious than she had thought.

"Well, I'm not going to Hell" Jada said.

"I wasn't saying that Jada. All I'm saying is, you need to make some changes in your life."

"Like what Maxie?"

"Okay. For one, you can't be going off on people and being rude just because. And secondly, you shouldn't be drinking and smoking like I believe you're doing. I smelled the smoke on you from time to time, but I didn't know it had anything to do with that club. I asked you about it and you said you were in the car with someone who was smoking. I had my doubts, but I decided not to say anything praying that the Holy Spirit would direct you and even me on when I needed to say something. I guess now's the time! I don't even want to get into the sex thing that I'm sure you think went over my head."

"What does all of this have to do with anything!" Jada said.

"You are always talking about how you read your Bible backwards and forwards. Well, if you studied your Bible backwards and forwards, and not just read it, you would know you can't be going to the club doing all that stuff you doing."

"See this is what's really bothering you."

"Actually Jada, all this bothers me. Do you even know what reveling is?" Maxine starts to pull out her Bible.

"Don't you dare pull your Bible out on me Maxine Taylor! I don't need you to show me nothing up in there. I know what's in there."

"Then you would know what reveling is. Reveling means wild parties or ungodly celebrations. When you go to these clubs you place yourself in satan's domain. You become subject to all kinds of temptations that your spirit has a hard time fighting off. When you go to the club, you're actually feeding your flesh. You cannot feed your spirit in the club while singing the devil's music, smoking, drinking and no telling what else you may be doing now. The Bible talks about all this in Galatians and Peter since you don't want me to show you." Maxine places her Bible back in her bag.

"Maxie, I know some Word too! The Bible also said in Galatians if you walk in the spirit you won't fulfill the lust of the flesh!"

Trina is watching them closely and she does not like the sound of this. She may not know what all these scriptures mean, but she remembers the pastor talking about how you shouldn't argue when it comes to the Word of God. Even she, the heathen knows that! Those two must've missed that sermon. Trina decides to stick her two cents in.

"Excuse me ladies, I could've sworn Pastor said somewhere in one of those two books of Timothy, that when you start disputing the Word of God amongst each other, you end up envious, suspicious, malicious, etc., etc., etc."

Jada and Maxine stop dead in their tracks and look at Trina out of surprise.

"Uh-huh, y'all be thinking I don't know nothin'. That should tell you—"

"Shut up Trina," Jada and Maxine say in unison.

"You probably just heard that on the radio or something," Jada said as she turns to Maxine. "Back to you!"

"No, back to you," Maxine replies. "You mean to tell me when you're in the club partying, drinking and smoking and doing your thing, you're walking in the spirit?"

"Well…yeah…to an extent."

"If you live in the spirit Jada, then you'll walk in the spirit. What you're doing ain't got nothing to do with the spirit. Now I know for sure you've lost it. You're not even the same Jada I've known. Yeah, you were always materialistic and self centered, but never did you compromise God's Word, at least not that I know of."

Trina laughs. "Well it depends on how you look at it. I've met a few spirits and—"

"Shut up Trina," the both of them say again.

"But… I—"

"Trina, didn't I say *shut up*! Nobody is in the mood for your corny jokes," Jada yelled. She's so upset with Maxine and her *oh-so-holy* attitude she doesn't realize how loud she has become. It's not like Maxie to be going back and forth with her about something she felt so passionate about. Maxie usually understood her and helped her, now she seems to be all into herself. She has a lot of nerve calling herself her best friend. Jada points her finger in Maxine's face. "He also said not to provoke one another, envying each other and that's what your problem is."

"What?" Maxine is quite puzzled at Jada's comment.

Trina senses that this is definitely the time where she needs to step in and end this argument. She takes hold of both of them by their arm. "Uh, Jada, Maxie, this is going a little too far. Let's not go there. Jada let's just go and do what we got to do tonight. I'm sure Maxie is busy tonight too. We can all get together later and talk when we've all had a chance to calm down."

"Oh no, we goin' there and we goin' there right now," Jada said. "*Little Ms.-Holier-Than-Thou* needs to hear this, all of this, and I'm not playin'!" Jada gets in Maxine's face. "You know, you've always been jealous and envious of me. I was the one blessed with a voice, not you. All I have to do is just whisper a song and people are falling out all over the place. You've hated and resented that from day one. You sit in that choir stand every single service with no one paying any attention to you. You want to know why? Because you're a nobody! No one comes to see you or even cares about you. No one! So why don't you just take your pathetic, little, non-existing, trying to be *Oh-So-Holy* self somewhere else 'cause you ain't got nothin' comin' here from me ever again!"

"Jada!" Trina cannot believe what she has just heard her say.

Maxine stands there in shock at the hurtful words of her best friend. Trina on the other hand realizing how far this has gone tries to set things back right between them before it's too late. "Come on now, remember me, the heathen. Even I, the heathen, know when you've gone too far. Jada, chill out! Please stop this, both of you. We're friends, home girls and y'all gon' make me cry. You know I don't like to cry because—"

Jada now turns to Trina. "No you listen too, *Lady of the World*. You be sitting up in the club acting like you so important, drinking all the free liquor before I even make it back to the table. You got everybody thinking that you manage me when you can't even manage yourself. You just hanging on my coattails because I make you look important. Ain't nobody here to see you either. Well guess what, I have a news flash for both of you so-called friends. I don't need y'all. I got somebody in my life and he's real good to me. He doesn't judge me or look down on me. And guess what! We're *handling* our business. Can you say that Maxine Taylor? Of course not! You know what? I don't have time for the likes of so-called friends like you two! So both of y'all can just step and leave me the hell alone."

Jada angrily walks away leaving both Trina and Maxine standing there dumbfounded.

"Now look at what you did Maxie. You're always upsetting her. You know how sensitive she is." Trina takes off running down the street toward Jada. "Wait Jada! Come on and get in the car. Slow down! I forgive you girl, you know you trippin'! Jada…slow down, you gon' make me break my heels."

All Maxine could do was stand there, losing the battle in trying to fight back the tears rolling down her face in full force. Angel pulled up alongside Maxine and blew her car horn. "Need a ride?"

Seven

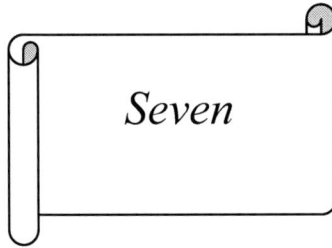

nother Sunday morning had come and the people flocked to Holy Tabernacle Church just to hear what words of inspiration Pastor Devine had from the Lord on this day. For the past few months the church had been packed. It was so crowded that he had to add another service with the possibility of adding a third. His technique of preaching sermons in series accompanied with music was a hit. But most importantly, the messages and songs appealed to the heart of the people, the heart of worship.

Not only was the congregation getting larger and larger, but the different auxiliaries were growing. The largest auxiliary had become the choir. The choir had become so large, they had to break them into groups just to cover all the services. With the increase of choir members, also came the increase in soloists. A number of good singers were coming to the forefront. Jada believed this explosion in the church membership was due to her and possibly her dual life. Some of the people she saw in the audience were the same people she saw at the club.

Pastor Devine had never approached Jada about her singing at the Wild Card and it had been a few months since she first started singing there. At this point, whether he knew or not, Jada really didn't care or even thought that he cared…as long as she did what was expected of her at the church. This was a true indication that Maxine had no clue of what she was talking about.

She missed Maxine. Maxine had called many times but she wouldn't answer. Maxine even tried to approach her at church but she would walk away. *Why am I acting like this?* she thought. Maxie was her girl, had always been her girl. And no matter what disagreements they had, she loved that… honest, radical, sweet, over-opinionated Maxie, who always had her back when it really counted.

Jada tried to place her focus back on the pastor, always being prepared to come out at any moment. He had been preaching hard and long. This series may be his best ever. She could see it in the faces of the people in the audience. There were a lot of tears on their faces.

There was one face in particular she couldn't help but pay attention to. He seemed changed for some reason or another. There was something different. It was like maybe an internal battle going on within him. But she really couldn't concentrate on that. She had to divert her attention back to the pastor. She couldn't risk missing her cue. There were way too many new people trying to take her place, which would never happen.

That was one thing she would not allow. No matter what was going on at the club or in her personal life, nobody would take her place. Nobody! They couldn't even come close to her talent. She knew it, Minister Peaches knew it, and definitely Pastor Devine knew it. But Pastor Devine was starting to scare her. In some parts of his sermon, it seemed like he was talking directly to her; without talking directly to her.

Pastor Devine was winding down his sermon. He seemed to be making an emotional plea unlike ever before. It was almost as if he could sense something in the air that was so ungodly; so menacing.

"Listen, people, I can't tell you enough, how important it is to get your life in order. We don't know the day or the hour when our Lord and Savior will come back. We don't know when our last day or hour shall be or when death will come. Please, don't let it come, don't leave this world and you're not ready.

"God only gives us one day at a time. What do you do with the day that the Lord has given you? Do you give it back to Him or do you give it to satan? Yes, satan. Any day that you spend not doing the will of the Lord, you're doing the will of the adversary. Take this day from now on and give it back to God. He loves you. He wants to spend some time with you. He wants to talk to you. He loves you more than you will ever know.

"Don't live in darkness and despair, envy and jealousy. Don't give another day to satan. He doesn't love you. He doesn't want to spend time with you or even talk to you. He could care less about you or your family. He already knows that he lost the battle, his only mission is to build up his army to prove the point he couldn't prove while he was in Heaven. The point he tried to make was that he was greater than his Creator. Can the creation of God be greater than the Creator? Is that what you want to serve? Satan wants to take away everything God gives you.

"But you see, what God has for you is for you. He blesses and gives you and me all different kinds of gifts. And no matter what we do with them, He does not take them back, no matter how we use them. Now that's an awesome God. Is there anyone here who wants to live this day…one day at a time…according to our Heavenly Father's Will?"

Pastor Devine stretches his hands towards the congregation.

"If you're tired of the mess, *Let It Go!* If you need a change, *Let it Go!* If people are misunderstanding you, mistreating you, walking away from you; *Let It Go!* Just let it all go and give it to God so that you can win. Tell me now…who wants to *Let it Go…* and *Let God?*"

Pastor motions to Minister Peaches while he extends his hands to the audience. Jada notices the slight nod from Pastor to Peaches. Jada begins to step out and Peaches places her hand against Jada's leg to move back in line with the choir. Jada is surprised at this action from Peaches. What's she doing? She has never done that before! Someone has to go out there immediately or the whole flow of the service will be thrown off. What could she possibly be thinking of? Pastor Devine is going to hit the ceiling. Heads are definitely going to roll on this one. Maybe this will work in her favor and Pastor will give her Peaches' job as Minister of Music.

Minister Peaches gives a subtle nod to Angel. Angel steps through the choir members to reach the podium. She steps up to the microphone and sings. And oh does she sing. People are swaying to the music as she cries and sings. The Spirit of the Lord has seemed to embody the words of the song. Her expression and body language appears to make the words of the song her own personal testimony. The congregation is feeling her and feeling the Spirit. People are being touched by the presence of God.

No she didn't call Miss Thang up there and in my place, Jada thought. Jada is hot. No, she's beyond hot, she's pissed. She can feel her temperature rising. She notices that a few of the choir members look her way and smile. Those haters! They all seem to think they can carry her torch. They can't even light her torch. She also notices that others are trying so hard not to look her way.

This whole ordeal had to be prearranged without her knowing. How could this happen? She never missed a rehearsal. She might've fell asleep a time or two, maybe three, even four. But still, no one ever said she could no longer sing. This was not good. What was even worse, the people were responding to Angel's singing. Well, it was her first time so they should at least pretend they like her! After all, that was the Christian thing to do.

But wait a minute there was something happening that was so much worse. The person in the audience she was watching earlier had his hands in the air, crying. He was actually crying. He left his seat and began walking down the aisle into the small group of people in the front of the church.

As Aaron's eyes are closed, he listens to Angel singing. He cannot stop the feeling he's feeling and is not even sure if he wants it to stop. He's been attending this church for awhile now and has never felt like this. He came close to feeling like this a couple of times before but he was able to shake it off, but not today. There's an amazing force in this place. Throughout the entire service he felt a pulling on him and is finally convinced that this is the Lord calling him. He becomes overwhelmed by the glory of God. Aaron comes down the aisle crying, kneels at the altar right next to Pastor Devine and gives his life over to the Lord as the people rejoice over another soul. Pastor kneels down with him and prays.

Jada can't believe what she's seeing. How is it, all this time he had been coming to church with her and he never came down when she sang? Why now? Maybe it has nothing to do with the singing. It couldn't be. Angel Buchanan was not even all that good. People had come down before Aaron, but once he came down, more and more people followed like the church was giving away money. It wasn't because of the singing, no way. Pastor was at his best and he really didn't need her in that capacity today. Plus Peaches probably knew she was dead tired and wanted to give her voice a break. She didn't think she needed the break, but she welcomed it since she was putting a strain on her vocal chords.

Focusing on Aaron has now made her forget all about Angel. Aaron coming down and joining the church was actually a good thing. She always said she wanted her man to be saved and in the church, and now he was. Jada smiled knowing that she and Aaron would be together forever. All things were working out so well. Everything was finally coming together. Just the way she had always envisioned it.

Eight

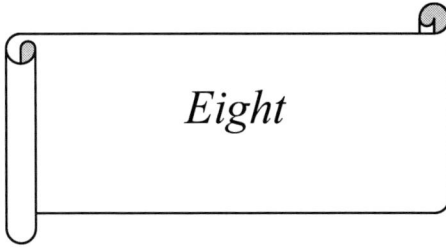

*J*ada and Aaron left immediately after the service was over. She was so excited that he joined the church and gave his life over to God she didn't know what to do. Her dreams were finally starting to fall into place. Aaron had suggested that they walk to Ms. Che Che's Place today before meeting with the others. It was such a beautiful day outside and he had so much inside of him that he needed to share. She on the other hand kept thinking about how all this started.

�֎

Ever since the first night Jada started singing at the Wild Card, Aaron had been at every last one of her performances. Ramón would always send over a bottle of champagne to her table, but she really didn't care for champagne. She drank it to be nice and mostly because it was there. Aaron knew she enjoyed a couple of glasses of chardonnay before each performance more than anything else. Then after the performance, she drank whatever it took to help her wind down so she could rest up for the next day. Aaron made sure whatever Jada desired was available. Jada loved that about him. The thing she loved most was that he was all about her, which was exactly the way she had always envisioned her relationship to be.

They began going out every night after her shows. Most times it was not a big date or anything like that, because they didn't get out of the club until about 11:00 at night. They would go somewhere quiet where they could talk more about each other.

Aaron had a lot going on in his life. He was single, never been married, and had no children which was rare for someone his age. He worked as an account executive with a brokerage firm and pretty much made his own schedule. His clients called him all throughout the day with financial needs and deals. You never saw Aaron without his phone and he answered all his calls. Aaron claimed his phone was his money and that was alright for Jada because he never stayed on the phone long. He had a way of professionally handling his business calls so that he could get back to showering Jada with all the attention he loved to give.

Their relationship became more and more serious. They were inseparable over the past few months. Aaron would leave her apartment around 1:00 a.m. in order to get back up at 6:00 a.m. He never complained about being tired. If she called on him, no matter the time of day, he was there.

She was becoming spoiled by all this attention. One late night, they were hugging in front of the fireplace at her apartment. Jada had become so comfortable with him. The passion inside of her for this man, was growing and growing. He kissed her on her forehead as he got up to leave. Jada was not ready to let go of him just yet. He was so perfect for her and she enjoyed being wrapped in his arms. She found herself thinking about him all throughout the day, each and every single day.

Jada grabbed his hand and pulled him back down to her. Aaron had never made a sexual move towards her even though it had been on both of their minds for weeks. They had never even discussed a sexual relationship.

Aaron knew her religious beliefs and wanted to honor that. He never placed any pressure on her. The passionate kisses they shared told a different story and left them both wanting more and more. Pastor Devine had always preached that there were three steps in establishing a relationship. First was the friendship, second, the fellowship and at last, the relationship. During that three step process, he also taught that couples should never touch each other. She might've missed a step in there but she now understood why there was a no touching clause.

But this was the night she had been dreaming about for some time. She had already decided she would give herself to him. Tonight, her conviction of celibacy until marriage was no longer important because she wanted him now. She wanted him more than anything.

He looked at her with much surprise. "Are you sure? I love you Jada and I never want to rush you. I want everything to be perfect with you and for you. I am more than willing to wait for you."

The more he said, the more he made her want him. She wanted this more than he did, at least that's what she believed and she was not about to turn back now. She had a few relationships before but the sexual temptation was never this strong.

Jada previously felt that waiting 'til marriage was really no pressure. In reality, it was easy to live a life of celibacy when there was no one in your life that you really wanted to share yourself with. But once that someone shows up, that's when the true test comes.

Well, it was pretty obvious that Jada was about to fail the test. She was not going to wait any longer. She was determined to have Aaron that night and she did. Jada never felt convicted or regretted a single day of making this decision.

✠

Jada stops reminiscing on their past time together, so she can focus on what's going on with him. Something's different about Aaron today, really different. The look on his face during the morning service was like no expression she could ever remember. Even more puzzling, he did not seem his usually affectionate self.

As they walked, he was silent and he still had that same strange expression. Jada thought it might be best if she opened up the dialogue. "What's with you today?" Jada was holding his hand as they entered the park. "When you came down that aisle you looked like a different person."

"You know Jada, I'm not sure if I can explain it to you right, but I'm gon' try."

"Oooh, this sounds serious, maybe we should sit down. Hold that thought 'til I find us a nice little spot." They walk further into the park. Jada spots a bench and leads Aaron to it.

Aaron tries to gather the words to explain his experience. "When I listened to Pastor Devine, his words began to light up something inside of me I cannot describe. Even when the young lady began to sing, those words were ministering to me as well. I became so full. I think that's the best way to describe the feeling."

"I don't think she was all that. Plus, I was the one who should've been singing."

"Jada, come on. Don't make light of that. I don't think you get it. It was not about the soloist, it was about the message. The Pastor's sermon was already pulling on me through the entire service, but when she sang the song *'Let it Go'*, right after he had been preaching that same message; that was definitely God's message to me and I knew it. For the first time ever, I felt truly loved by God."

"I remember when it was like that for me. That was such a long time ago."

"Jada, I began to see pieces of my life and I was not happy with what I saw. I always felt like something was missing in my life. It has always been like something was drawing me to the church. I actually thought it was you."

"I would like to think it's still me." Jada smiles and pulls him close.

"Don't get me wrong, you've played a real important role in all of this. I had visited the church before … *like the night we met* … but it was actually my relationship with you that kept me coming back. The problem was, I was coming to the right place, but for all the wrong reasons."

"But that's okay Aaron. When God has a plan, we never really know how we're players in that big picture. The thing that mattered was that you kept coming with me. And the more you came and hung around me, the more the Word would get into you, especially when I sang."

"No Jada. It wasn't about you, it was about God. You were just the one He used."

Jada senses the seriousness and the change in him. "What are you saying?"

"This thing between us has been wonderful. I've enjoyed you from the moment we first met, however..." he pauses trying to choose the best words for this situation, "...I'm saved now and I don't think this is the road I want to travel."

"This *thing* between us! Not the *road* you want to travel? So now our relationship has been diminished to a *thing* and I'm a *road* you traveling down!"

"I didn't say that. I'm not even saying I don't want to be with you. I just don't want to continue to live like this... in sin. I've given my life over to God this afternoon and all the things I've done that aren't right, I cannot continue to do them anymore."

"Wait a minute Aaron! We can't still see each other anymore? How you gon' stop everything just like that? All this because you're saved now? Your salvation has nothing to do with our relationship!"

"Are you kiddin' me? Jada, how can you say that? Our relationship has a lot to do with this! You've been in this longer than I have so I would think you would understand what I'm dealing with here."

"That's why I know all this ain't necessary. We've already crossed that bridge of intimacy. It doesn't make sense to go back across and act like it never happened, because it did. And I've enjoyed every minute of it." Jada softly outlines his lips with her finger.

He pulls her hand down. "Jada that's not fair."

"I'm not trying to be fair. I'm just trying to love you."

"I can't do this." Aaron turns away from her.

Jada takes his arm and pulls him back around to her. "Aaron, I'll tell you what…I do understand and I'll compromise. We can still spend the night with each other and enjoy each other, but not be intimate. It might be hard in the beginning, but we can deal with it."

"Deal with it? We can't do that! If we put ourselves in those situations, things will happen. I guarantee you, things will happen! I may be a babe in Christ but I know that the flesh ain't no joke to deal with. My flesh is strong for you, Jada. I already know what it's like to be with you and that will be on my mind all while I lay next to you. And I can tell you right now, I am not that strong. Look, I've been in sin a lot longer than I've been saved. We just need some time to let God make it happen and stop making it happen for ourselves."

"But I love you Aaron."

"I know baby, I love you too…and…but…now we both love God…but this doesn't seem right!"

"And what does that mean?"

"It means He'll let us know what our next steps are if we just pray about it. Right now Jada, I need to concentrate on Him to find out what I need to do. But don't worry. Really, this is not a—"

"Why is everybody getting so holy all of a sudden and making it seem as though my services are no longer needed? Or maybe I'm the one with the problem. Maxine has been acting a fool and left me. Peaches knows I sing when the doors of the church are opened and she puts in little Ms. Perfect Angel! And now you want to dump me!" Jada pauses for a moment to take this all in and then gets up from the bench and starts walking. Aaron gets up and follows along behind her. "We're all Christians now, right Aaron? We're all living for the Lord, am I right? So why all of a sudden everything needs to change from what we've been doing?"

"Jada, I don't make the rules. I've only been saved and committed for just a little while and I'm not about to act like I know it all or have all the answers. There are things I don't understand, I will admit. But what I've noticed is that people confess Christianity all the time. But these same people don't live a day in their life as you would think a Christian should live. After all, I thought being a Christian is to walk, talk and at least try to live like that of Jesus Christ. Am I right about that?"

"Yes, but—"

"But just because you do a few good things in your life, you're automatically bound for Heaven? I know it's got to take more than that! What happened to the commitment to, the relationship with God and living the example Jesus has already set? Aren't we supposed to think about…" Aaron is snapping his finger, trying to think of that Christian cliché he hears all the time. "…Oh yeah I remember, '*What would Jesus do?*' What about that?"

Jada stops and turns to look at him. "Now I'm the one who don't understand this one. So now, *you're* the expert on Christianity! You now know how to live the Christian life and Christians don't?"

Aaron takes Jada's hands in his. "It's not like that and you know it. I'm talking about me right now, Jada… me. If I'm going to be a Christian, then I got to do this thing right. Once I commit to something, I gotta go all the way. First I got to learn how to live saved and then learn how to stay saved." Aaron pauses. "Jada, I'm not judging you, I know you and to know you is to love you. I think you…I…we…should start taking a deeper look into our lives, our walk with God."

Jada pushes his hands off of hers and looks at her watch. "Oh no you didn't, *Mr. You-So-Holy!* You been saved all but two hours and now you gon' tell me how to live my life. I cannot believe this. I got more holiness in my baby finger than you will ever have in your entire soul."

Aaron steps back and looks at Jada. He has never seen this side of her. "Maybe I'm not saying this right. I'm trying to say—"

"You're definitely not saying this right! But fine! You don't need to say anymore! I don't need you or anybody else to tell me anything! Enough is enough and I've definitely had enough! How you gon' tell me about me! Let me tell you about me! I am a living, breathing, walking, talking, saved soul. I don't need you or anyone else questioning my actions as a Christian. God anointed me to sing, *me*! When *I* sing on Sunday, do you see how *I* reach the people? Do you see how they become slain in the spirit when *I* lift up *my* voice? Do you know how many souls have come to God just based on *me* and *me* alone? Little Ms. Angel will never be able to accomplish that! *I am* the true example of *Holiness*! Now you can take your rotten, good for nothing, two hour *holier-than-thou-attitude* and get the *hell* outta my face! Just like I told Maxie, I don't need you or anybody else in my life."

"Wait a minute Jada you're working yourself up for nothing. I'm not dumping you, I—"

Jada takes off running to get away from him. She's hurting so bad from what he has said and becomes blinded by her own tears. Jada immediately stops when she hears the sound of a car horn. She turns around. Aaron is calling out her name but she can't hear him. All she can hear is the sound of tires screeching on the pavement as she stands there frozen.

Nine

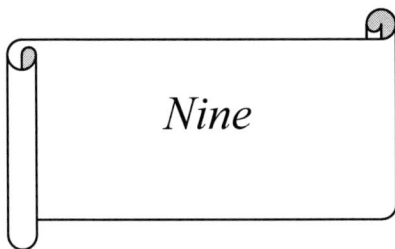

*I*t had been a long day and James was worn out. There had been two morning services and he had been there all day attending both of them. As soon as Pastor had the altar call, James slipped over to where Ellie was sitting and whispered for her to get LJ to the car as soon as service let out. He wanted to make a quick getaway before anyone else said they needed something that would tie him up longer than he wanted. These double services were taking its toll on him, and Pastor had the nerve to talk about adding a third one. But if that's what it takes, he'll just have to suck it up because nothing will ever keep him from doing his job in the church. All he had to do for now was to tie up some loose ends and he was out of there.

In spite of the long Sundays, the Addams family was in such good spirits. Things had been looking up. Everything was going good at the church, at the job, and at home. James had been promoted to a higher level position at work. Ellie had received a pay increase at her job so she hadn't cried broke in a while. Plus she was secretly trying to pay off some of those bills James didn't want her to pay. Paying the bills made her feel a little more comfortable. She had been taught if you made the bill, you paid the bill.

It seemed as though once they both started making more money, they also began winning a little more with the lottery. Actually, the winning increased because they were purchasing more tickets. Ellie felt if they could buy more tickets, they could pay more bills. She was the one who wrote the checks for the bills, purchased the lottery tickets and collected the winnings. James' only role in this was to provide the money and the numbers that Ellie played.

Even though they won a little more often, they still lost more; way more than they ever won. But that didn't matter. James didn't see this as a loss. He saw it as all part of the master plan. You win some, you lose more. But in the long run, you win it all.

James finally made it to the car where Ellie and LJ were waiting. Ellie was behind the wheel thinking he would be too tired to drive. He starts to loosen his tie and then opens the car door. "Ellie you know it ain't respectable for a man to be chauffeured by no woman. You get on over to the other side."

"You look so beat, I just thought—"

"That's awfully nice of you hon, and I appreciate it but a man gotta be a man. This is not your job so move on over." Ellie obediently slides over to the passenger side.

James gets in and rolls down his window. "Why y'all sitting in here with the air on. We don't need the air on today. Ellie, roll that window down. It's a beautiful autumn day and I could use some fresh air. By the way, did you pick up those tickets this morning like I told you? They're going to announce the numbers soon so you need to find a radio station. Maybe a news station or something like that."

"Don't worry James, I think I know one." Ellie rolls down her window and starts fumbling with the radio. "In between the services this morning, I ran out and played the numbers with the money you gave me."

"Good girl, yeah, it's a big one today. It's the biggest one ever so let's cross our fingers." He looks back to see LJ sitting in the back of the car with his legs folded on the seat, reading his Sunday school book. "Roll down them windows LJ. Let some fresh air in back there too. I get tired of the air conditioner, especially on a beautiful day like today."

"Okay," LJ says. He places the book on the seat and rolls both of the windows down. "I'm hungry dad, can we stop and get something to eat?"

James pulls away from the church. "That's exactly what we gon' do because I'm starving too. We gon' run by Ms. Che

Che's Place real quick. I already called in the order, so it should be ready by the time we get there."

"Let's go to the park and eat," LJ said.

"Why would we eat in the park?" James asked.

"Actually James, that's a good idea. Like you said, it's beautiful outside and that would really be relaxing after such a crazy day today. You know the park has a table and bench area where you can eat or we can just lay a blanket down. It's one in the trunk."

"Alright, alright, we can do that, plus it will give me a chance to unwind." He looks through his rearview mirror and sees LJ still sitting with his legs folded on the seat, reading. He notices his shiny shoes for the first time. "Put your seatbelt on little man and by the way, are those another pair of new shoes your auntie got you? Ever since that first pair, we can't seem to get her to stop. I didn't get a chance to talk to her after service. She's so busy with that big choir now. I did get a chance to talk to your cousins, but only briefly."

"Yes sir," LJ answers but continues to read his book.

"You've been pretty busy too," said Ellie. "You have more responsibilities with the extra service the pastor has added. Looks like he has been adding new assignments to everyone."

"Yeah, but we family, and we still need to take time out for each other. No matter what, we family. I told her boys to come on by with her today after church. I don't get to spend much time with them boys and they need a male figure around from time to time. They said they were going to play some ball and will see us later on." He looks again in his rearview mirror at LJ. "LJ, did you see your auntie today?"

"I saw her at the children's church. She said she came down 'cause I was in her spirit and she wanted to make sure I was alright."

"Did she see that you were wearing your new shoes?" Ellie asked.

"She sure did. She said we would definitely talk later."

James yawns and stretches as he tries to hold on to the steering wheel. "What you two be talkin' about all the time anyway?"

"Well auntie tells me to say my prayers and talk to God every morning and that I should start my day by saying 'Good Morning Lord'. She said if I can speak to my parents every morning when I get up, I should do the same to God since He's the one who really gave me the day. Then she said, do the same at night. But of course I would say 'Good Night Lord' instead of 'Good Morning Lord'. You know dad, Auntie Peaches said God would reveal what tomorrow holds for me since you won't tell me."

James lets out a hearty laugh on that one. Even Ellie joins in on the laughter. "Oh don't pay no mind to your Auntie Peaches," James says. "She just tryin' to be funny. Plus it don't take all that praying to get through to God. He knows your heart so most times you don't have to even open up your mouth. All that conversation is just not necessary. I mean it ain't gon' hurt, it just ain't all that necessary."

"But dad, she says the only way to have a relationship with someone is to talk with them and spend time with them. And she says God is no different. He's real jealous, and all He wants us to do is love Him, talk to Him, and follow Him."

"That's a bunch of nonsense. I got a relationship with your mom here and we don't talk or spend time together and we're just fine." He turns to Ellie. "Ain't that right Ellie?"

"That's right! Now listen to your dad LJ."

"That's right. Now Ellie, find the station before we miss the numbers. Wow, I can't believe that boy remembers everything Peaches tells him." Ellie continues searching the stations. "By the way, we gon' cut through the park and go to that gas station on the other side of Ms. Che Che's Place. I need you to run in and get some cigarettes, I'm all out."

"Sure James, no problem."

"Dad, Auntie Peaches says when you smoke you're destroying the house the Holy Spirit needs to live in. Is that true?"

"Nope! God didn't say nothing about smoking in that Bible. I know that for a fact because I looked it up and couldn't find it. What's that woman teaching you?"

"She said we supposed to give our bodies to God as some sort of sacrifice and if we do anything on purpose to mess it up, we're committing a sin. When you drink dad, is that a way to mess it up on purpose too?"

"Look boy, you talking a little too much. Ellie, make sure you remind me to ban that sister-in-law of yours from our house. Forget everything I said earlier about family. She's starting to fill this boy's mind with a lot of nonsense and I'm not gon' have it!"

"Yes James," Ellie finally finds the station. "Here it is," she listens for a moment. "I think they about to read off the numbers now." She reaches in her purse and pulls out the tickets.

The radio announcer comes on. "Okay listeners. These are your winning lottery numbers for today's million dollar jackpot. That's a six hundred sixty-six million dollar jackpot. Good Luck! Okay, the first number is twenty-five."

Ellie starts shuffling through the tickets to find any of them with that number on it. "Oooh we got a few with that number."

"Quiet girl before we miss the numbers," James said.

The radio announcer continues. "The next number is fifteen."

"Oooh we got fifteen."

"The next number is nineteen."

"My God James we got nineteen."

"Quiet woman 'til they finish!"

"You ready folks, the next number is three…and the last number is nine."

"Oh my God, James. I think we got it."

"What you mean you *think* we got it? Ain't no time to think, it's time to be sure!"

"Okay listeners; listen again while I call all the numbers in order for that next lucky winner. The winning numbers are 3-9-15-19-and 25."

Ellie starts to scream and waving her hands around scaring the mess out of James and LJ. "*We got it, James we got it!*" Ellie is screaming and waving the ticket around so hysterically that the ticket comes loose in her hand and is blown around inside the car because all the windows are open.

James grabs at the ticket. "Ellie! Whatcha doing?"

In all this excitement, LJ is on his knees jumping up and down already celebrating. He looks out the front window past his mom and dad and sees a woman running out into the street. "*Dad …Dad…there's—*"

James turns just in time to see what LJ is yelling about. He pounds his horn and tries to brake. "*I'm not gon' make it,*" he yells as he sharply turns the wheel to his left! His first reaction is to throw his arm up to keep LJ from flying up to the front since he knows he did not have on his seat belt. He hears a slight bump as the car goes into a spin. He yells, "*Ellie, hold on*", but she cannot hear him above her own screams.

Ten

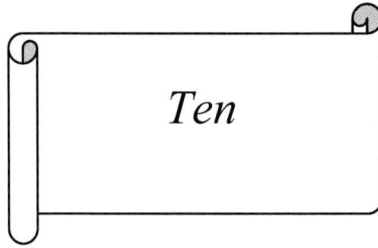

*F*ifty new members joined the church that day and the members were rejoicing. This was the most that had ever joined at one time. There was definitely an explosion in membership at Holy Tabernacle Church and this kept many of the church workers busy. This was a tremendous blessing for Pastor Jon Devine. His prayers had been answered and all because he had followed the plan God had given him. God had shown him a way to get to the hearts of the people.

Pastor created a new auxiliary and named it *God Squad.* Their purpose was to serve as security for the church and help control the flow of people, which was a direct result of the increased membership. Their duties also included watching out for members going in and out of the neighborhood. Some members were reporting problems with some of the neighborhood so-called gangs. Pastor Jon Devine wanted his people to feel safe and have a sense of security when they came there to worship or work in the different ministries.

Joshua and Jacob were assigned to the God Squad. They were also given additional duties which kept them constantly in direct contact with the pastor and his ministerial staff. Joshua and Jacob were finished with their assignments and decided to wait for their mom outside, in front of the church. It was such a beautiful day. While outside waiting, Maxine came out to talk to them.

"Hey guys, how're you doing?"

"We're fine Sister Maxie," Joshua said. "What brings you out here?"

"Yeah, is mom finished up in there?" Jacob asked.

Maxine hugs the boys. "Oh no, not yet. It was actually your mom who sent me out here."

"Okay, what's going on now?" Joshua says.

"You know how hard your momma works with this ministry and Lord knows she is such a perfectionist. But she said if you guys wanted to wait she will be through in a couple of hours."

Jacob looked at his watch. "I don't mind waiting."

Joshua looked at his watch as well and looked up at Jacob. "Man, you must be smokin' somethin'. You know if mom says a couple of hours it'll take at least three to four."

Maxine nodded. "Yeah, Jacob, I have to agree with your brother on this one. It may not take that long, but once your mom starts working on a project, she becomes consumed and time no longer has a limit or relevance. And I'm sure you all understand why she stays so busy with all that has happened."

Joshua looks down the street, not looking at anything in particular. He allows his mind to wander on the events of the past which had caused a dramatic change in his family. "We do understand. Even though she's handling things a lot better now, we still see from time to time when she becomes totally preoccupied and we know why. What do you suggest we do Sister Maxie? Should we wait or go home?"

"Well, if you want to wait about another hour, I can drop you off. I'll definitely be leaving way before your momma."

Joshua thought about it for a moment. "We might as well just leave now. We can take the bus home, plus it's nice out here today."

"Yeah, that's cool," Jacob agreed. "Sister Maxie, could you tell mom we went on home?"

"Are you guys sure? I don't mind if you don't mind."

"Nah, by the time you finish up in here, we could be at home playin' ball. I wanna go shoot some hoop today anyway. I need to show this turkey some of my new moves," Joshua said. Joshua hits Jacob upside his head and starts to shuffle his feet as if on the basketball court. Jacob joins in and the two of them act like they are playing ball.

"Okay you two, no problem. But y'all be careful. You know the problems we're starting to have around here with some of the boys in the neighborhood so watch out. I can take you to the bus stop, if you want."

"Sister Maxie, we are not babies. We can walk to the bus stop. Remember we're the *God Squad* of the Holy Tabernacle Church. We're invincible, nothing can touch us," Jacob said.

"You're already touched," laughed Joshua. "I don't know by what, but you're definitely touched."

Maxine laughs at the boys' playfulness. "Just make sure you call your mom on her cell phone once you get home so she won't worry about you. Let me know that you made it home safely too, if you don't mind. Think you can do those things for me since you are agents of the…*God Squad*?"

"Will do! See you later Sister Maxie," Jacob said.

"Bye Sister Maxie."

"Bye boys." Maxine watches the boys as they playfully walk down the block. She really loves those two. They had been through so much. As a family unit, they were tight. She thought back on her family and friends. Her family was fine but her relationship with Jada was very strained. She tried to talk to her, but Jada refused to talk. Trina said she just needed to give her some time. She had also suggested that she just show up at the club and that would probably help to heal Jada's wound. But no matter what, Maxine knew she wouldn't compromise that part of her for Jada's insecurities. She headed back into the church once she could no longer see the boys.

Joshua and Jacob took off for their short five block walk to the bus stop. It had been months since that last incident with the neighborhood boys and they hadn't thought about it too much after that. A block before they made it to the bus stop, Tiny and his boys came running from around the corner.

"Well, well, well," Patch said. "Look Tiny. Guess what we got lurkin' around in our neighborhood."

Tiny stops behind them. "I just know that sweet lil' ole couple didn't have the nerve to show their faces back in our neck of the woods after we gave them a break. I honestly believe they came here lookin' for us!"

Joshua and Jacob try to ignore the boys and keep walking. Tiny and his boys begin to circle around them.

Patch stops Joshua and Jacob from walking when he stands in Joshua's face. "I guess they didn't believe us when we warned them. This one is always looking like he's ready for a fight. This is the one I want."

"Do you think maybe it's time we show these church boys just how serious we are over here?" taunted Tiny. "We've been trying to send some messages to that church over there that they ain't welcome here. Oh, I get it now, they sent these two to show us the error of our ways."

"Let me show them Tiny. It's my turn anyway."

"Naw, Patch. This is kinda special and dear to me. You see, that church over there is just another building full of hypocrites that turn their noses up to people, especially people like us. They think they so much better than everyone else, especially since a whole lot more people are goin' there now."

Jacob is amazed at his thoughts of their church. "Now wait a minute! Where're you gettin' that from? That's where you're wrong man. It's not like that at all at the Tabernacle."

Joshua doesn't particularly care what the guys think about the church. "Don't say nothin' to him! He could care less what we do at the church or how we are."

"No, by all means, say what's on your mind," Tiny said to Jacob. "Hey guys, we got us here a young preacher man who wants to preach and tell us about *the Lawd*. So let's let him preach. All y'all pull up around preacher man and let's see what the *Word is from the Lawd*."

"We're not lookin' for any trouble," Joshua said. "We go to church over here and now we on our way home. We ain't here to preach or to judge. We not even here to fight."

Tiny moves over toward Joshua. "Who was talkin' to you?" He inches a little closer to him. "I asked you, who was talkin' to you? I said we gon' let preacher man preach. If you got a problem with that then it's just too bad. Now you shut up or we'll shut you up!"

Jacob thinks he might be able to calm them down and get through to them at the same time. "Look man, you got us all wrong. Somehow we got off on the wrong foot. You seem to have it in for the church. Can I ask you why you hate the church so much?"

That question alone incensed Tiny even more. He did have an issue with the church, not just that church but all churches in general. What the boys didn't know was that Tiny was not always Tiny—he used to be a PK—a preacher's kid. His real name was Antonio Dixon. His father was a prominent minister back in the day. Not only was his father a senior pastor, but he was over the entire religious order of churches in their faith. His mom and dad worked faithfully within the church organization for years. Both of their entire incomes came from the church, because that was their full time job. They were dedicated to their faith, their church and their members. Antonio was brought up in the Word of God and knew it better then most people in the churches, even now. But one day, everything changed. Everything changed and so did the rest of his life.

"You can't ask me nothin'!" Tiny pokes Jacob on the shoulder. "You here to tell me somethin', preacher man! You here to tell me why I'm going to Hell. Why I gotta pay for the error of my ways. Why I need to turn my life around. You not here to ask, you here to preach! Now preach!"

"Man I ain't no preacher and I ain't here to condemn or judge you either. Can you tell me somethin' man? Can you tell me why you so bitter against us? We've never done anything to you that we know of. If we can help you, let us know. I don't have an aught against you."

"Well I got an *aught* against you. It's not the church I hate, it's people like you in the church. Most of y'all don't even live in this neighborhood. You just come over here like we invisible and go back to your upscale neighborhoods like we never even existed. I thought the church was supposed to help people, especially the people in its community. There are people right here on these blocks that don't have food to eat and barely have clothes to put on. What y'all do for them?"

Jacob believes he's getting somewhere with him. "We can accommodate our ministry to meet your needs, that's what we do. Someone just needs to tell us what they are. We have food drives and rummage sales all the time. All the people need to do is just come."

"Yeah right, that's what you think. I've been to a few of those. The food cans are rusted and you sellin' the clothes, you ain't givin' them away. If the people had the money to buy the clothes, they would go to the stores and maybe even some thrift shops, not to y'all! So all you do is give us old food that you don't even want and stained cheap old-fashion lookin' clothes. How do you think that make us feel?"

Sensing that this subject is probably more personal to Tiny than he wants to let on, Jacob tries to reason with him. "You know, I never thought of that, but that's why we need people like you to come over and talk to us. Tell us what your needs are so we can work with you, not against you. We have people in the neighborhood working with us in the church. Maybe you and some of your guys can come and work with us. You need to help us help you."

"So now he wants to work with us," Patch said. "Why we doing all this talkin' Tiny? Let's just do what we need to do. We've already talked about what we would do to them if we caught 'em again."

Joshua realizes that this is not good and pleads with his brother to let it go; not understanding what Jacob is trying to do. "Jay! What you doing man? Let's go! They don't care nothin' about us and they've already made up their minds about us. At this point, it's either do or die and frankly I'm ready to do."

"Wait Josh, calm down. Let's see what we can do for them. Maybe we have been insensitive to their needs."

"I'm tellin' you, they don't care nothin' about us, this is a set up, bro'!"

Patch has gotten annoyed with Joshua. "You know Tiny, this one has really gotten on my nerve. Since you said do or die, then check this out!" He grabs Joshua around the neck, pulls out a gun and holds it to Joshua's head.

Joshua puts his hands in the air even though now he's more pissed than surprised. Jacob freezes when he sees the gun up to his brother's head.

"Why you gon' pull a gun on me?" Joshua is furious. "I ain't got no weapon. Let's just handle this one-on-one. I tell you what, you put the gun down. You and me, one-on-one. You said you don't like me, that's fine, 'cause I don't like you. But we can handle this like men. Just you and me, nobody else, and no weapons."

"Josh, stop it! Just shut up!"

Tiny looks over at Jacob. "You see, that's always been your brother's problem. He don't know when to shut up. He got a gun up to his head held by my boy here who's a straight up fool, and he still want to talk mess. Who the fool?"

"Please man, don't hurt my brother. You and me, we talkin'. My brother and I can be of help to you and your partners. That's what our church does, it helps people. We believe in the power of God. I know that God can turn this situation around. He can work this out for you, for me, my brother and your guy there. None of us have any control here.

God has the control and He can change everything for everyone here."

"Yeah, I used to believe that garbage too. But, is that supposed to be your sermon? I've heard way better than that. Matter of fact, I can do better than that and I ain't even in the church no more. You gon' have to do a little better than that, plus…the picture looks fine from where I'm standing. I can't say the same for your boy over there."

Jacob catches that phrase from Tiny about no longer being in the church. "Look, I know you already know somethin' about the Lord and somethin' may have happened to make you feel this way, but I'm not here to preach to you man. I'm just here to tell you that the God I serve loves each and every one of us, no matter what we've done or what we'll do. You, Patch, your boys, it don't matter. He does not love me any more than He loves you. All He wants is that you come to Him, seek Him, and give your life to Him. Whatever's in your life that has gotten you all messed up on the inside, just let it go man and give it over to Him. Once you do that, I promise you, your whole life will be changed. You'll be a whole new creature and all this you're doing won't be important to you any more. And what's even better, God won't hold it against you, you will be completely forgiven and the best thing about that is, all this will be completely forgotten by God! Come on man. Who really cares what other men think, it only matters what God *does*."

Joshua is not paying attention to Jacob and Tiny. He and Patch seem to be having their own private conversation going on. "Man you need to get that gun outta my face!"

Patch turns Joshua around and faces him with the gun still up to his temple. "And if I don't, what you gon' do punk! You always talking that mess. You've no idea what we go through out here! You don't know nothin' about struggles!"

Jacob hears the interchange going on between Joshua and Patch, becomes alarmed and gears his conversation to Patch. "You're absolutely right man; we don't know what you have to go through from day to day. But we can all work this out together. All you have to do is—"

Patch turns his attention to Jacob and slightly loosens his grip on Joshua. Joshua takes that as Jacob diverting his attention in enough time for him to react. Joshua seizes that moment, quickly shifts his body back and grabs at the gun. Joshua and Patch fight for control of the gun. Joshua is trying to kick Patch while holding on to the gun. His boys stand back not knowing what to do because they know the gun is fully loaded. Then all of a sudden, the gun goes off. Everybody freezes not really knowing in what direction the bullet has gone.

Jacob falls to his knees.

Once Joshua realizes his brother has been shot, he knocks Patch to the ground and runs over to Jacob. Patch, who still has the gun, gets up and points the gun at Joshua who's leaning over his brother.

Tiny grabs Patch by the arm. "No, just go man! Go! Go now!"

Patch continues to grip the gun and aim at Joshua. Tiny steps in front of the gun. "Did you hear me? I said go!" He yells to the other guys, "Get him outta here! Y'all know what to do, so just do it!"

One of the guys runs up to Patch. "Come on Patch, let's go man before someone calls the police." Patch and the boys take off running.

Tiny stays and stands there for a moment looking at the two brothers. He walks over to where Jacob is laying on the ground. Joshua is crying and talking to him, trying to help him up. Tiny looks down at Jacob. "You know! He almost had me. Yep, he almost had me." Tiny shakes his head, turns and takes off running.

Joshua is pulling at Jacob, trying to get him up, screaming for help.

"*Somebody Help Me! Please!*" He yells and positions Jacob to perform CPR. "Come on man, get up. You ain't gon' let no little bullet get you down. You always said God has the master plan, so come on man and get up." He yells again for help and goes back to talking to Jacob and trying to pump air into his lungs. "You got a life to live, Jay. Don't give up. Don't you dare give up! Remember, Pastor said you will live and not die. You supposed to be a preacher and I'm supposed to be your Armor Bearer." Joshua begins to cry uncontrollably. He stops and looks down at his brother. "I'm supposed to take care of you. Come on Jay, don't do this to me! This is no way to pay me back for me not being there with you and dad. This is not right. It wasn't my fault. Don't do this to me. Just think of mom, Jay, just think of mom!" Joshua continues to try to keep him breathing but there's so much blood.

The sound of the gunshot causes Paul Olsen, one of the church members who lives in the area, to look out his window. Once he sees Jacob and Joshua on the ground, he calls 911. He hangs up and calls the church. Maxine answers the phone. "Miss Taylor, this is Paul Olsen, I need to talk with the pastor, something has happened. I'm not sure what it is, but I think I heard a gun shot and two of the boys from the church are on the ground. I think one of them has been shot, but I'm not sure yet."

Maxine realizes the boys were walking in the direction of Paul's home. "Oh my God, no. I'll go get Pastor and we'll be there right away. Call the police."

"I already called, but I'm about to go out there with them to see what I can do," he answered and hung up. He immediately went outside where a small crowd of people were already gathering.

Maxine gets on the intercom to page Pastor Devine, security and of course, the boys' mother. They all, including some more church members, jump in their cars and drive to where the boys are. Peaches makes it there first. She sees Joshua on the ground holding Jacob with Mr. Olson kneeling next to them. She immediately jumps out the car.

Paul sees her and runs toward Peaches. "I called the police and the ambulance is on their way. They should be here any minute. It doesn't look good Minister Peaches."

She nods at Paul not really listening to him, but continues to run past him to where the boys are. Pastor Devine pulls up right behind her with Maxine and Angel in the car.

Peaches reaches the boys, kneels down next to Joshua and takes Jacob in her arms. "Joshua what's wrong with your brother? What happened here? Are you alright?"

Joshua looks up to her with tears in his eyes and blood all over his hands and clothes, not really able to speak.

Peaches panics when she sees the blood. There's so much blood. Angel and Maxine make it to her side and try to calm her once they see the blood. "Josh, what happened?" Peaches yells at him. "Tell me now, what happened?" Joshua is still unable to speak.

Pastor Devine reaches them and immediately checks Jacob's pulse while Peaches tries to prop him up against her chest. Pastor places Jacob's arm down and tears begin to stream down his face. "Peaches, I'm sorry. He's gone."

"Nooooooooo!" Joshua yells. "Nooooooooo!"

Peaches pushes Pastor, Maxine and Angel away from her and Joshua, and pulls Jacob closer into her bosom. "No, what you talkin' about Rev! You obviously don't know nothing about the power of God." She holds him close to her rocking him back and forth. "This is my son, my baby; and ain't nobody gon' take him away from me. He ain't gone no where! God has big plans for him. You will see, you all will see. This boy has got a life assignment. He gon' be a preacher just like you Pastor." Peaches is crying and hugging Jacob real tight. "You see Pastor he's just getting started. You'll see, you'll all see. I'm telling you, he's just getting started."

Joshua is hugging his mother from behind crying. "Mom, it's all my fault."

She reaches one arm behind her to hold on to him as well. "You hush up now Josh. Ain't nothing your fault! Don't you ever talk like that! I don't want to ever hear you say that again! Don't you worry, everything's gon' be alright. Don't pay them no mind! They ain't God! And God ain't go let your dad and Jacob be taken from us." She rubs Joshua's head and turns her attention back to Jacob. "I thought someone said they called the ambulance."

Pastor Devine takes the hand of Maxine and Angel and begins to pray. They in turn take the hands of the other church members standing next to them. Like a chain reaction, all the people standing around, follow suit and take the hand of the person closest to them. They build a solid wall of prayer around the distraught Wright family. Everyone's crying and praying as the ambulance and police cars pull up. The people break open their wall of prayer to allow help to get to Peaches and her sons.

"Come on Jay, my precious baby, it's not your time," says Peaches softly as she continues to rock Jacob and hug Joshua. Joshua is crying so hard that his eyes are swollen almost to the point of closing. Peaches just continues to softly talk to her baby boy. "You can do this. You're strong. Don't pay any attention to them. They don't have our faith. This is not the day for you to leave us." She holds Jacob up to her chest.

The paramedics try to get to Jacob but Peaches can't seem to let him go. One of the paramedics takes his arm to get a pulse while the other uses the stethoscope. They look at each other shaking their heads to confirm their findings to each other and the police officer standing by. The police begin to direct questions to the people still in the wall of prayer. Peaches notices the sign the paramedic gave to his partner. She begins to loudly lament. *"Lord please, please don't take my baby, Lord please, no. It's not time yet."* Jacob still does not move, Peaches screams at the top of her lungs. *"No Lord, Not Again! Not My Baby! NOOOOOO!!!!!*

Eleven

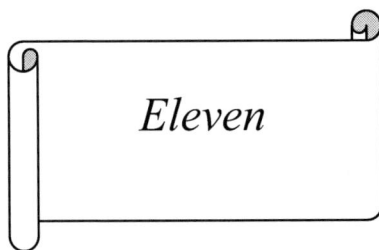

*T*here was dead silence. It was almost as if he was watching a terrible horror movie. The day started with him turning his whole life around and then there he was, standing on the corner arguing with the woman he loved dearly about his transformation. He couldn't get her to understand his point. She ran away from him and then there was a car horn and screams. He couldn't remember if the screams were his or hers. He vaguely remembered seeing things flying in front of him but couldn't quite place or even remember what it was he saw. Everything happened so fast. But now, there was only dead silence.

Aaron blinked as he looked around. He could've sworn she was just standing here. Where did Jada go? He was the only one standing there now. Maybe she fell to the ground in an effort to dodge that car that was blazing down on its horn and tires just screeching. He had to find her so he ran into the street to look around. There were no other cars anywhere, with the exception of the parked cars. For such a beautiful day, there wasn't anyone in the park but them. This was so strange, but nevertheless, he had to find her.

He then saw the car that was honking its horn. It had spun out of control and hit a pole on the other side of the street. Oh my God, there was debris all over the place. He couldn't even make out what it was. He ran over to the car to see if the people inside were okay. He didn't' see anyone. Good thing too because the car was a mangled mess. But if they weren't inside, where did they go? They must've crawled out while he was looking for Jada. It just didn't seem as if there had been enough time. Had time just stopped? Perhaps they found Jada and took her to safety. But how could that be? This place was pretty much deserted and he would've had to see something.

No one was in any of the parked cars. He started looking in between them to see if Jada and the other people were possibly propped up against one of the cars. As he peeked between the cars, he saw a shoe. Aaron froze. It looked just like Jada's. She would never leave her shoe behind, never.

He moved around to the side of the car, that's when he saw her. It all started to come back to him. She was on the ground, lying halfway on the curb and halfway on the grass. This is where she landed after being hit by the car. He remembers yelling her name when he saw her run into the street in front of the car. The driver blew his horn and tried to turn the car but there was not enough time. Jada ran from between some parked cars and there was no way he could've stopped in time. The next thing he remembered was Jada being lifted in the air, something else flew across his face and then he went blank.

Still not able to move, he looked at her lying on the ground. "Jada, Jada, are you alright?" She didn't answer. She didn't move.

He immediately pulled out his cell phone, thinking to himself...*I should have done this a long time ago, what's wrong with me?* "Operator, this is an emergency. I need help right away!"

"Yes sir, what's the nature of your emergency?"

"There's been an awful car accident. My girlfriend...she's not moving." As he talks to the operator, he realizes the enormity of what has happened and he begins to sob into the phone, still frozen in place.

"Okay sir, I am sorry for what has happened but I need you to be as calm as possible. Can you tell me your location?"

"I'm close to the corner of 55th Street and Payne Dr. in Washington Park."

"Alright sir, I'm dispatching emergency teams right away. How many vehicles are involved?"

"Only one." He looks at Jada's twisted body lying on the ground. He couldn't believe this was the beautiful young woman he was just having a conversation with. More like an argument. "She didn't see the car coming before she was hit. Please hurry."

"Are there any other people with injuries?"

"I don't know. The car lost control and hit a pole. Oh my God, let me check." Aaron runs back across the street. He now realizes what was flying in front of him when he went blank. It was not debris from the car, but the actual passengers. He cringed at the bodies he saw lying in the street. "Oh my God operator, they were ejected. They're lying on the street. This is so horrible, please hurry."

"How many are there?"

"There are two people and they're not moving. I think they're dead. Oh my God, oh my God." He heads back over to where Jada is lying.

"Okay, don't move anyone. The ambulance and Fire Department have been dispatched. Are *you* alright, sir?"

"No… no I'm not. But I'm not injured either. Please, just hurry."

"They should be pulling up any minute now. Would you like me to stay on the line with you? We need you to stay at the scene until help arrives."

"Don't worry. I will never leave Jada."

Aaron closes his phone as he moves to sit next to Jada. Why would she just run out like that? Could this all be his fault? Could he have driven her to this blind run into the street?

He picks up her hand. "Jada, can you hear me? Speak to me. Move your finger, something." Jada does not respond. Aaron holds her bloodied hand up to his face. "I'm so sorry. It wasn't supposed to happen this way." He looks up in the air and begins to yell. "Lord, please…forgive me. I've caused this, I'm so sorry. This is my fault. Have mercy on me…on her. Please Lord, bring her back. Don't let this be her last moment. Not like this. Give her another day to do Your Will." He bows his head crying.

Above his own sobs, he hears the faint sound of someone crying out for help. Aaron jumps up immediately and runs toward the direction of the voice. He passes by the lifeless looking bodies in the street. Oh no, he sees a young boy still trapped in the badly mangled car, seriously injured. How could he have missed that before?

"Help…me…pleeease! Mom…Dad, where are you?"

Aaron kneels down next to the car and reaches in to grab him. "Hold on little man, I'm going to try to pull you out. Hold on to my hand." LJ weakly reaches out for Aaron's hand. "Okay, on the count of three, I want you to try to lift yourself while I pull you free. You think you can do this?" LJ nods his head, yes. "Okay, one, two, three." Aaron tries to pull him out, LJ yells out in pain. "I'm sorry, I'm sorry, I'm not supposed to move you. Can you move or wiggle your way out? You seem to be sandwiched between something, I can't seem to tell what it is."

"I'm trying…it's not working. Oooh, I can't do this…it hurt too much."

"Okay little man, you're wedged in there pretty good, but don't worry, I've called for help. They're on the way. Don't try to move anymore. Let's just wait for help." Aaron hopes they hurry up, he doesn't know what to do.

"I hurt…so much… Mister."

"I know you do, but just hold on. I'm going to stay here with you until the ambulance gets here."

"Thank you. You seen…my mom…dad?"

Aaron looks over to the two people lying in the street. He cannot bring himself to tell this little boy about the two people lying in the street, who are apparently his parents. He tries to change the subject. "Was it just the three of you in the car?"

"Yes, but…could you…find…for me, let 'em…know… where I'm at, so… won't worry…about me?"

"I don't think they would want me to leave you. I'm going to stay right here with you until you don't need me anymore."

"Sir…why…this happen? Uhhh…it hurts…it hurt so bad!"

"Just take it easy and breathe slowly." Aaron lowers his head in disbelief. "I don't know. I don't know why it happened like this. It all happened so fast." He raises his head and tries to change the subject. "What's your name?"

"L...J."

"LJ?" Aaron takes a closer look at him. "I know you. I'm Aaron, Sister Jada's friend." Aaron looks over at Jada and then at LJ's parents lying on the ground. He remembers Jada waving to LJ and his mom as they were sitting in the car back at the church. "Oh my God, I can't believe this is happening. Don't you worry LJ. You're going to make it, you're gon' be just fine."

"Think God needs me...Heaven...more...He... here?"

Aaron notices that LJ is not totally coherent. "Don't talk like that, you're going to be just fine. I know it. I want you to relax now."

"Mr. A...I can't feel... pain anymore..."

"Are you sure? Try to stay woke, whatever you do, LJ, do not close your eyes!"

"Maybe ...God took pain away... put it on Himself...just like...Pastor said." LJ begins to cough, blood running down the side of his head and his arm. He looks up at Aaron who has tears rolling down his cheeks. "Don't cry Mr. ...my auntie always said... you get in something...you not...able to get out..., remember...God loves...God loves you...much...He sent Jesus...He the One...who really went through the pain for us. Maybe...it was Jesus...who took the pain away...put it on...Himself."

LJ starts to cough uncontrollably and spits up blood.

Aaron hears the siren of the emergency teams. "Don't talk anymore LJ. Please, save your strength. Help is coming. Hold on, just hold on. God does not need you in Heaven. I need you here, my little brother. You can never know how much I need you, I need you so much right now. Your mom and dad would want you to hold on. Imagine how they would feel if you gave up. You mentioned your aunt. I'm sure she would want you to be strong. I know it's hard but you can do it. I promise you LJ, you can do it!"

The emergency teams have arrived. A paramedic runs to where Jada lies while another one to LJ's parents. Another team of paramedics come to where Aaron and LJ are. They can't get to LJ because of the way he's pinned down in the car. They yell to the guys from the Fire Department to bring tools to cut him from the wreckage. While the firemen are working to free LJ, the paramedics place an oxygen mask on LJ. One of them gives him an IV with two liters of saline solution. They instruct Aaron to keep him talking.

"Auntie said…God…loved…world…would give… forever … if you just… if you just…" LJ can't seem to get his thoughts together. He takes a deep breath. "I love Him…do you…Mr. Aaron?"

"More than I've ever loved Him before." LJ's hand goes limp and Aaron panics. "No please, no! Do something, there's got to be something you can do."

The paramedic looks up to Aaron "Your son?" Aaron shakes his head. The paramedic continues, "I'm sorry man. He's gone, probably from massive internal bleeding and there's nothing we can do. We can't even get to him from the way he's pinned in there."

"But he's just a child."

"I know. That's when this job really stinks. From the look of it, none of them had on their seatbelt. I'm sorry man. He's gone."

Aaron gets up and staggers to the middle of the street falling to his knees. He looks up at the sky, "God, why take an innocent child? Why this family? Why Jada? Take me Lord! Take me!"

Emergency teams are all over the place surveying the accident site while other paramedics are trying to work on the victims. All of a sudden, one of the paramedics yells out, "Over here! We got a live one! Let's get 'em out of here!"

Twelve

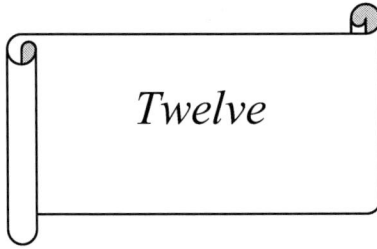

There's total darkness. There are no sounds. There appears to be no signs of life. All of a sudden flashes of light illuminates the room for mere seconds at a time. LJ appears, sitting in a chair tossing and turning. It seems as if he is in a deep nightmarish sleep. He can hear familiar voices.

James Sr.:

Oh, don't pay no mind to your Auntie Peaches. Plus it don't take all that praying to get through to God.

Peaches:

You know God loves you, don't you?

Just say 'Good Morning God'.

Ellie:

You know, you're the most precious thing to me in this whole wide world.

Peaches:

God will direct your path in time. Don't worry about tomorrow. Today is all that matters.

James Sr.:

Alright little man. You go with your auntie and have some fun. Me and your mom, we love you son.

✠

LJ fades into the darkness. James Sr. appears. He's sitting in the same chair tossing and turning appearing to be in a nightmarish deep sleep. He can hear familiar voices.

Peaches:

You know about the Lord. You go to church every Sunday, you and your family.

Ellie:

We only use the money for lottery. What about paying our tithes? I can't even remember the last time we paid tithes.

Peaches:

You're a leader in the church so therefore you must be an example to all the others who are under your leadership or who just look up to you.

Pastor:

For He also said in His Word "I've set before you, life and death, blessings and curses; therefore choose Life that you may Live!

Peaches:

'Thy word have I hid in my heart that I might not sin against thee'. You have to read the Word in order for it to get in your heart so that you can live the Word.

Pastor:

But let me tell you my *peoples*; if you don't give ear to the voice of the Lord, then *curses*; I said *curses* will come on you and overtake you.

Peaches:

Believe it or not James, eventually you will have to take a test, so I suggest you read the Word so that you can pass.

One Day…This Day!

Pastor:

God only gives us one day at a time. What do you do with
the day the Lord has given you?

✠

James Sr. fades into the darkness. Jacob appears in the
chair tossing and turning in a deep nightmarish sleep. He can
hear familiar voices.

Tiny:

Maybe we'll just come and pay y'all a visit over there at
that little church. Maybe you can save us too.

Joshua:

You gon' be a preacher or something?

Tiny:

That church over there's just another building full of people
that turn their noses up to people like us.

Joshua:

You sure you ain't gon' be no preacher?

Dad:

Promise me you'll take care of them!

Tiny:

It's not the church I hate. It's people like you in the church.

Joshua:

Somebody got to watch out for you… and I do believe that
I'm the person for the job.

Tiny:

You know; he almost had me!

✠

Jacob fades into the darkness. Jada appears sitting, tossing and turning in a deep nightmarish sleep. All of a sudden the familiar voices start again.

Ms. Che Che:

You're sending mixed signals. That's why the world is so confused on religion.

One Day…This Day!

Trina:

I too am a nice person. Matter of fact, I think I'm better than you. You just cursed out the man at the grocery store.

Maxine:

I really believe if you do this, it'll be like trying to serve two masters.

Angel:

You have a beautiful voice. God has really anointed you.

Pastor:

Don't give another day to the devil. What God has for you is for you. He gives us all gifts and no matter what we do with them, He does not take them back, no matter how we use them.

Ms Che Che:

You're showing the people we're trying to reach that it's okay to be a Saint at church and an Ain't everywhere else.

Aaron:

We need some time to just let God make it happen and stop making it happen for ourselves.

Maxine:

My voice may just be the last one you hear.

Jada disappears. There's total darkness. There are no sounds. There appears to be no life. The voices can no longer be heard.

Thirteen

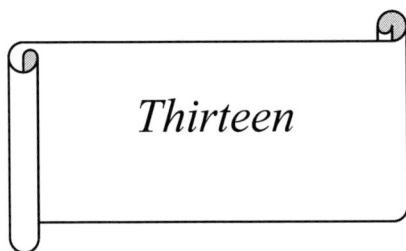

*L*ights once again illuminate a gigantic room filled with rows and rows of long benches and a couple of desks and chairs located inside what appear to be small stands or maybe even podiums. Each one is pretty modest looking, located on opposite sides of a spectacular podium of some sort. The podium appears to have large golden jewels carved right into the most magnificent grain of mahogany wood. There are other stones as well, but none like any that have ever been seen before. The stones and gold jewels together illuminate a bright and magnificent light. An enormous empty chair is set inside this grand podium and it too looks as if it's made of that same mahogany wood. The matching chair has the same jewels accenting the outline of the head rest.

The podium and chair stand about ten feet high. It's truly magnificent. It would take a really big person to even fit in that stand. And if they could fit, the light from the stones would be blinding. This had to be a showcase of some sort, because it looks too brilliant for just anyone to occupy. The chairs and stands on both sides of the podium dull in comparison, almost looking out of place.

All rows of bench seats are completely occupied with people, but none of the people are moving or talking; everyone seems to be in a daze. One of two seats up front is occupied by a man that seemed to just materialize from nowhere in particular. He sits at the rather small and obscure stand, very emotionless and still. He almost appears to not breathe.

There's a calmness about this place. It's neither cold nor hot. The air is still and it has no smell.

Jada slowly looks around the room trying to understand her surroundings. "Where are we? I just had the craziest dream," she whispers to the person next to her. Jada looks up and does a double take. "Hey, I know you!" Jada looks at the other people next to him in amazement. "Wait a minute; I know you and you too!"

James Addams Sr., James Addams Jr. and Jacob Wright are all sitting there together. She's happy to see some familiar faces but is still puzzled. "Where are we and how did we get here?"

James Sr. seems to be happy to see her as well. "Well I'll be damn if it ain't the little songbird. I wish I could answer your question but I can't. The last thing I remember was I was driving with my boy, LJ here and his mom when some crazy lady jumped out right in front of my car. I tried to hit the breaks but she was too close so I swerved to keep from hitting the fool and my car went into a spin. Next thing you know, I was in a room hearing voices."

"You know what," Jada said. "As I think back, that was like the last thing I remember. The only difference is, I wasn't driving but I was running to get away from someone when all of a sudden, I looked up and saw a car coming right at me. I completely froze."

James looks at her suspiciously. "Wait a minute…don't tell me…"

"Daddy that was Sister Jada you hit. I saw it all."

"Impossible! No…are you sure? She couldn't have been that crazy lady running out in the street like that. Could you?" James asked turning towards Jada.

"I sure couldn't have been," Jada said. "For one, I'm no crazy lady. And two, I was not hit by a car, look at me. Do I look like I've been hit by a car?"

Jada and James Sr. look at each other. "Wait a minute," James said. "Even if I did hit her and my car went into a spin, how did we get here?" James looks across from LJ. "And by the way, what's your story?"

"I'm just as confused as you are Uncle James," Jacob said. "But my story seems to be different from yours."

"Are there anymore people here from the church? James said slightly looking around. "Matter of fact, where's your brother and your momma? I know she got to be in here somewhere. It's just like her to get lost in the crowd. She's probably sittin' back there running off at the mouth when she needs to be up here with her family. Ellie's probably back there with her."

Jacob stood and looked around the room. "Well I don't seem to recognize anybody else in here." He sits down and turns towards them. "But like I was saying Uncle James, the last I remember is Joshua and I was walking to the bus stop after church when some guys came to start a fight."

"It use to be so quiet and peaceful there." Jada said.

"Yeah, there're some problems there with some of the locals. Joshua and I got into it with them before."

"Wait a minute," Jada said. "Is that the same incident I was trying to talk to you two about before?"

"Yeah, that's right. We just didn't want to make a big deal out of it. We probably should've told. But anyway, I remember Joshua got into a fight with one of them who pulled out a gun."

"A gun! They pulled out a gun on Joshua?" LJ said. "Knowing Joshua, he probably got real mad. Did they try to hurt you too Jay?"

"I don't think so, but not only did Joshua get mad, but he jumped the guy who pulled the gun out and they began to wrestle for the gun."

"That sounds like Joshua too," James said. "Your momma would just lose her mind if something happened to one of you boys, considering y'all just lost your dad. You and Joshua alright?"

Jacob stands up again to see if he sees Josh. "I don't know where Josh is and I'm fine, at least now I am. I remember feeling a lot of pain and then just like that, the pain left. Then I was in darkness seeing scenes of my life kinda flash before me."

LJ reached up and hugged his cousin, Jacob. "You know what, I'm glad you're okay. I was in a lot of pain too, just like you were. I was talking to Mr. Aaron, you know Mr. Aaron. He's Sister Jada's friend."

Jada perked up when she heard LJ mention Aaron. "Aaron! You talked to Aaron, LJ? How? When?"

"I don't really know. I was in a lot of pain and he was talking to me and then the pain stopped. And just like Jacob, I was in the dark and could hear and see you all talking to me. You all were saying things you already said to me before. It was weird."

"Yeah, I'm with you LJ," Jada said. "This is too weird. The question is, how did we all get here together? I couldn't have gotten hit by you James because I feel fine and I'm still here. I never experienced any pain."

"But I saw you Sister Jada," LJ said.

"You saw me what?"

"I saw you run in front of the car. I tried to warn my dad, but I think he hit you anyway."

"That's nonsense, LJ. You couldn't have seen me. There was no way that could've happened."

"Well you have to admit one thing," Jacob said. "Something is definitely going on in here that we can't seem to explain. What's even worse, I don't know where Joshua is and momma gon' have a fit if we're not together."

James pats Jacob on the leg. "Don't worry about it too much nephew, you here with family. I'll talk to your momma when I see her."

LJ looks around the room when all of a sudden, the brightest, most magnificent lights never seen before, begin to shine all around them. LJ looks at the others. They are totally speechless and in awe of this incredible light. He smiles the biggest smile ever. "I know where we are."

Once the light enters the room, the small man dressed in all white, sitting in the small stand right next to the grand one, stands up. He walks out of his podium to the center of the room. "All rise!"

Immediately, all the people rise on his command. With all their confusion, they didn't know what else to do or what was really going on, with the exception of LJ it seems.

After they all stand, the lights begin to take form. The form becomes the appearance of something huge in a long white beautiful robe. The face was so unbelievably handsome, youthful, with a touch of wisdom and confidence. The form appears to have likeness as that of a judge, but there's something distinctively different about this judge. Not only is the appearance beautiful, young and wise, but a look of peace and yet sadness.

The light doesn't completely leave the room. The Judge seems to come out of the light and yet still be a part of the light; for the light continues to shine all about Him. He approaches the magnificent desk and sits down.

"You all may be seated," the small statured man said. Everyone obeys.

Jada whispers. "LJ, you said you know where we are."

"Yeah," James Sr. said. "Where are we boy?"

Jacob looks at the judge. "I think I finally understand too."

"What?" James Sr. asked. "What you understand?"

The small man in white spoke again. "Silence in the courtroom, please. You'll all have your turn to speak."

James and Jada looked at each other. "Courtroom?" they say together.

181

"James," Jada said. "I think we're dead. And…oh my God… this is our judgment!"

'No Way!" James looks confused.

"That's exactly what this is," Jacob replied.

"Let me explain the format for these proceedings," the Judge said. "Each one of your names will be called. You will come up to this empty stand here on my left. You will answer the questions put forth to you…if you desire. I want you to be comfortable and not intimidated by my bailiff here or by my presence. This is your opportunity to say whatever you like. You will not be judged or punished for what you say here. What has been done is done. This is your chance to come into complete understanding. This is your time to shine or burn—"

"Your Honor!" the bailiff said.

"Oh yeah, well, bad choice of words. Okay this is your time to tell things about your decisions—good or bad, your choices in life and how they pertain to how you lived. This is your moment. But first, I need to bring everything back to your remembrance. You are only remembering the final bits and pieces of your life at this moment. That will all change now." As the judge speaks, everyone begins to remember the events of their entire lives.

The Judge looks down at His list with the names of every soul in the room. "Looks like it's going to be another busy day, so let's get started. Bailiff, call the first defendant."

"Yes, Your Honor!" The bailiff turns toward the souls in the courtroom. "Please come forth when your name is called." He looks down at his list of names. "I call James Eugene Addams Jr. to the stand."

LJ looks around the room and then looks at his dad. "I think he's calling me. Is it alright, dad? Should I go?"

"I think it'll be alright. You go right ahead. I'll be here if you need me. All of us are here, so don't you even worry."

"I'm not worried dad, I think everything will be alright." LJ rises and walks to the front of the courtroom. He smiles as he approaches the bailiff.

The bailiff pulls out the Bible. "How are you son?"

"I'm fine sir."

"That's good. The Judge will ask a few questions and I need you to respond to him truthfully. Can you promise to do that?"

"You bet sir. My auntie said it don't pay to lie cause God knows when you're lying. She said He hates a liar and one couldn't even stand in His face." He pulls the shirt of the bailiff to come closer and the bailiff leans in. "That Judge looks like He could be God so I know I will be good just for Him just like my Auntie Peaches always said.

The bailiff smiles at LJ and looks up to the Judge. "Your Excellence, I present to you James Eugene Addams, Jr. affectionately known as LJ."

"Thank you bailiff. James Addams Jr., you may take a seat right over here." The bailiff shows LJ where he should sit and returns to his seat as the Judge looks over an enormous book located on his desk. "Alright James, or should I call you LJ?"

"You can call me LJ if you don't mind, I kinda like that."

"Very well, LJ. That's what I shall call you." He looks back into The Book. "Okay, I see that in your very few years of life you have seen and heard a lot."

"Well, I guess so, but I don't think I understand, Sir."

"I see that you've been raised in a Christian home. In this Christian environment, you've seen lots of acts which have caused you some confusion."

When James Sr. hears that, he jumps to his feet. "I object."

"You can't object, Mr. Addams. This is not your life," the bailiff said.

"But that's my son, and to imply confusion at home would be a direct reflection of me. So I indubitably object."

"Sit down Mr. Addams," the Judge said. "You are not able to answer what is in his thoughts or his heart. I will allow you your time to speak, but only for you and your life. That's a promise and I'm known to keep my Word." James sits back down and the Judge turns back to LJ. "As I was saying, have you been able to understand what's right and what's wrong according to God's laws?"

"Oh yes Sir, Your Honor. My mom and dad took me to church every Sunday and I loved it. Sometimes there were things the pastor would say that I didn't understand, but my auntie would always sit me down with my cousins. That's my cousin Jacob over there." LJ waves to Jacob. "Like I said, she would explain what the pastor was saying to make sure we understood."

"You loved your Auntie Peaches."

"Do you know Auntie Peaches?"

"I sure do."

"Of course you do. My Auntie Peaches was always very good to me. So were my mom and my dad."

The Judge looks back down at His book. "There's really not much to go over here, mainly because you've been a wonderful example of how a young person should live his life. And you are considered as innocent in the eyes of the Lord. Many adults could've learned something from you if they had opened their hearts and minds to you. You listened, you learned and you responded."

"But why did I die? And the way I died? It hurt so bad, at least in the beginning!"

"Listen son, good people die all the time. They don't always get to lie down and go to sleep and then just wake up here for judgment. There are times that tragic events happen to make a change in another area of your life or someone else's life that you may not understand or ever see. You tried to warn everyone of the impending danger but it was too late. However, before you died, a young man was with you who had just given his life over to God. He was trying to figure out how to deal with some internal and external struggles in his life…"

Jada begins to cry when she hears the Judge and LJ talking about this man that had been with LJ. She messed up big time with Aaron. If she had just listened and not been so defensive, none of them would probably be here today. Her actions set off a chain of events that affected each of them with the exception of Jacob. But luckily for her, she had been a Christian and served God for most of her life. Her whole life was about servitude. At least her life's work would make up for a few mistakes.

"…He held you and talked with you trying to get you to hold on but there was no need for you there anymore, and I think you knew that. Your life assignment had been fulfilled at that very moment. Your words and your pain in that tragedy, changed Mr. Aaron's life forever. It eventually made him a strong believer. He travels all over the world teaching the Gospel. He tells the story of that one moment you two shared as his opening to all his teachings."

"But the pain?"

"You tell me about the pain."

"Well actually, it seemed as if as soon as I began to really feel the pain, it was gone."

"And why do you think that is?"

"Because Jesus took it away?"

"Good answer. Why do you think Jesus took it away?"

"Because He already done the suffering for everybody, at least that's what my auntie would always say."

"She's a wise woman. In your last moments, you were trying to say something. Do you remember what you tried to say after the pain went away?"

"Yes, I remember. Auntie Peaches used to say that God did this just for me. I couldn't get all the words right because I was getting so sleepy."

"I knew what you were saying. Normally it's the job of the bailiff to quote the written Word as it's recorded in the Bible. But LJ, this time, could you do it for me, for all of us? Tell everyone here, what you were trying to say with your last breath."

"Yes Sir, God, I mean Your Honor. I was saying *'For God so loved the world that He gave His only begotten Son, that whosoever believeth in Him shouldn't perish, but have everlasting life'.*"

"Bailiff, tell LJ where that scripture is found."

LJ becomes excited and raises his hand. "I know, I know!"

"Okay LJ. Then you tell the courtroom, where that scripture is found."

"John 3:16."

"Did you believe God? Did you believe God loves you so very much."

"Yes Sir I did … I still do."

The Judge smiles at LJ. "Good, I'm glad." He continues to ask LJ more questions until He has discussed all the things needed to be covered. "LJ, you may return to your seat. Bailiff! Call the next soul."

Fourteen

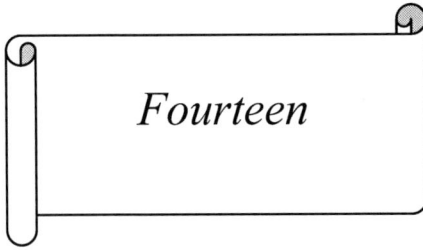

*T*he bailiff turns to the souls in the courtroom to announce the next name. He looks at his list. "I call James Eugene Addams Sr. to the stand."

James Sr. stands and walks toward the stand. LJ stops once he reaches his father. James Sr. stoops down and gives him a big hug and directs him to his seat by his cousin Jacob. James Sr. continues on up to the stand for his turn at judgment.

James is feeling pretty good about this whole judgment thing. After seeing how everything went with his son, with the exception of that one remark, he felt more assured than ever before. Once he reaches the stand, he climbs up one step to the seat and turns to face the bailiff who's waiting for him. The bailiff holds the Bible against his chest.

James notices how the bailiff holds the Bible and becomes a bit confused. *That's not how they held it on Court TV*, he thinks to himself. "What you want me to do? Raise my hand, swear or something?"

"Oh no sir. We don't swear here. This is a holy place. However, you may speak freely. Do you promise to give truthful accounts of all events you will be questioned on, telling the truth and nothing but the truth?"

James raises his right hand. "Yeah, of course. I ain't got no reason to lie."

"You can put your hand down," the bailiff said. "That's not necessary." James puts his hand down. "Are you familiar with this book, Mr. Addams?"

"Of course I am."

"Have you read this book?"

James nervously pulls at the loose tie around his neck and glances up at the Judge. "Uhhh…yeah!"

"Is that the truth or are you lying already, Mr. Addams?"

"Will that count against me?"

The bailiff looks up at the Judge who slightly nods his head. The bailiff opens the Bible and reads. "Proverbs 6:16-19 says, *'There are six things the Lord hates: and seven are an abomination: A proud look… a lying tongue—*," the bailiff looks up at James as he emphasizes lying tongue. *"Hands that shed innocent blood, a heart that devise wicked imaginations, feet that runs swift to mischief… a false witness that speak lies,"* once again he looks up to James.

"Your Honor, I object! Why he keep doing that? Why he looking at me like I'm guilty of that?"

"Bailiff, please continue to read. And do not look at Mr. Addams like he is guilty of that," the Judge said.

"Yes Your Honor." He continues reading. "*...and he that sows discord among the brethren.* Do you recognize yourself with any of these characteristics, Mr. Addams?"

James thinks about this for a moment. "I don't think I'm gon' like you."

"That's okay, I'll ask you again. Have you read this book?"

"Well...," James pauses and scratches his head. "...I kinda, sort of...skimmed through the pages from time to time if you want me to be more technical."

"Are you a Christian, Mr. Addams?"

"Yes, of course I am. I'm also the head deacon in my church. My sister and I handled all the affairs of the church. And I want to let you know that I was good at it too."

"But you haven't read this book."

"Now, now, don't be so hasty. You're getting me all frustrated up in here. I am a man of God and I know what's expected of me. I'm always at the church and I'm there for the people. I follow all the rules of the church and do what my pastor tells me to do. So that should make everything alright!"

The bailiff turns the pages. "It says in 1Peter 4:17, '*for the time has come that judgment must begin at the house of God*'."

"And your point is?"

"You haven't read this book, Mr. Addams. A yes or no answer will take us to the next question, unless you just don't want to answer. If that's the case, it will be acceptable."

"Hey, slow your role, Mr. Bailiff. Let me explain. It's like this, I've never been much of a reader—everybody knows that. I was a hard worker and didn't have time for no reading. My pastor did all the reading and studying. That was his job. He was there to break it down for the rest of us. Ain't no sense in me reading, if he gon' read and explain it to everyone. My job was to just listen and follow."

"So you don't have any first hand knowledge of any words in this book?"

"Well it's like I said—*and you got to pay better attention to me when I talk*—I skimmed through the pages from time to time when I needed to. I can't quote you anything but I know the Word when I hear it."

"*Thy words have I hid in my heart that—*"

"Yeah, yeah, yeah. I've heard that one before. Let's just move on."

"Alright, so once again, have you read this book? A yes or no—"

"I know, I know. A yes or no will take us to the next question." James mulls over what he should say. "I'm getting tired of this line of questioning cause you ain't listening, but if I must answer like you want me to, then the answer is…No!"

The bailiff looks up to the Judge. "Your Excellence, we have a soul here proclaiming to be a Christian and, I must add, he has not read the Word."

"Whoaa…wait a minute, Mr. Bailiff! What you mean proclaiming to be a Christian? I am a Christian. You know, you and me, we're not seeing eye to eye here."

"Mr. Addams, you must understand, I'm not the Judge and I don't make judgments against you. My job is to present your case to the Judge based on your words, not mine; your words of acknowledgment of the Bible. Then I am here to tell you the Word of God as it relates to your case. *You* must plead your own case. The Judge will have the final say. I am but a servant."

"Okay, okay, then that's cool. If I may translate, to make sure we have an understanding. What that really means is I don't need to deal with you anymore 'cause what you say really don't matter." James wipes his brow. "Whew, you had me worried for a minute. This should be easy now. Heaven here I come!"

The bailiff looks up at the Judge shaking his head but smiling. "Your Excellence, I hand over to you, Mr. James Addams Sr. for judgment."

"Thank you bailiff. Mr. James Addams Sr., you are definitely the lively one. And how would you like me to address you?"

"Well…Mr. Addams seems kind of formal and a little impersonal. And more importantly, I want you to be comfortable here with me. So why don't you just call me James."

"Alright James, and once again, you are welcome to speak freely. Now the bailiff tells me that you're a proclaimed Christian. Is that so?"

"Oh no Your Honor. I ain't no phony saint like some of them other people in the church. I'm the real thing."

"Alright James, please, plead your case! Tell me about your life as a Christian and what you've done."

"Well, you see Your Honor, it's like this. I joined Holy Tabernacle Church when I was about thirteen years old. I went to church every Sunday from the age of thirteen on up into my adult years. I was a faithful and diligent member of the Holy Tabernacle Church. Because of my dedication to the church, I was chosen to be on the deacon board and eventually appointed as head deacon. Did I say that I never missed a day of church? Oh yeah, I think I did say that.

"Well, I was right there on the front row for every service. I was good at handling the business of the church, no matter what it was. Everyone knew Deacon Addams or DJ as they called me; that of course stood for Deacon James. Yeah, they all knew me and my family. Yes Sirree, Your Honor. I was faithful and diligent. I was at church every time you even thought it was going to be a service. I was dedicated. My works and dedication to the church proves that I am what I say I am, a true Christian."

"And while you were there every single service for the numerous years of your life, sitting on the front row, working in your ministry and in your church, how many people did you bring in?"

"Bring in? What do you mean; bring in, Your Honor?"

"I mean, how many people are you responsible for bringing into the knowledge and salvation of Jesus Christ? How many people did you witness to about Christ? I mean this James, how many people became knowledgeable of your beliefs, because of you?"

"Knowledgeable?"

The Judge looks at the bailiff. The bailiff opens the Bible. "*My people are destroyed for lack of knowledge—*"

"Oh yeah, wait a minute, I know this one and I know exactly what you're talking about. That scripture right there is in the book of..." James is thinking hard trying to remember what book of the Bible that scripture is found in. He snaps his finger. "I know, I know. It's Josia...or something like that. Now let me think about this knowledge thing for a minute or two." James starts thinking of people and trying to count them on his fingers. "Well umm…let me see, there was errrr-ummmm, let's see…there was Ellie; that's right Ellie. And ummmmmm, of course LJ! Okay. Okay. Ummmmmm…that's it. Ellie and LJ! That's him sitting over there. You talked to him already." James points to LJ. "Funny though, I can't seem to find Ellie."

"So you're saying your wife Ellie, and your son, LJ!"

"Yeah that's it. That's two souls that wouldn't have come into the knowledge and…what you say earlier? Oh yeah, the knowledge and salvation of Jesus had it not been for me."

"So you're saying, from the age of thirteen to present, you have brought two people into the knowledge of God."

"Well two people would be better than none, don't you think?"

"What do you think, James? You tell me," the Judge said.

"I did the witnessing thing in the beginning when I first got saved and I don't remember if anybody even paid attention to me. It ain't my fault Your Honor if they don't listen. It kind of all fell off later on when I became so busy in the church. But I know one thing to be true though Your Honor, and that's Ellie and LJ came in through me. Ellie didn't know nothing about nothing 'til I came along. And of course I had to raise LJ because you know the Bible says to train up your child in the right way in the Lord and he won't forget it, he might stray, but he won't forget." James turns towards the bailiff smiling. "See, I can quote some Word too!"

The bailiff smiles back.

"Well, well James," the Judge said. "If nothing else, that was an understanding of the Word taken from Proverbs 22:6. An understanding is what matters most. And speaking of understanding, there's no book in the Bible named Josia. The book was Hosea. Now let's keep going." He looks at His massive book again. "You're saying that you're really not sure how many people you witnessed to about the Gospel other than your wife and son...or maybe you just didn't witness?"

"I guess, Your Honor. I really ain't done none of that. That was for other folks like missionaries, evangelists or something like that. That was really not in my job description. I was about the business and operation of the church."

The Judge looks down at the bailiff. "Bailiff."

The bailiff turns the pages of the Bible. "Mark 16:15, *'Go into the entire world and preach the Gospel to every creature'.*"

James tries to peek over into the bailiff's Bible. "That's in there? Well I'll be!" He tries to straighten his tie. "Well you see Your Honor, that's one of them situations where my pastor didn't tell me that... directly. So, how was I supposed to know I had to do that if he didn't tell me? I think you need to get him here so we can start questioning him. Now he should know better being a man of the cloth and all." James is still pulling at his tie nervously trying to straighten it. The happiness he felt earlier about being able to quote a scripture is swiftly taken away.

"James, if you had read your Bible, you would've known for yourself. Let's go on."

"Beg your pardon, Your Honor. Wait one minute and let's not go so fast, please Sir. I used to read at times. I had to do that so I could get my deacon moan on. Let me show you real quick." James stands up and does a rendition of his deacon moan and some of the souls sitting on the bench quietly snicker at him. Once he finishes, he sits back down.

"You got to be kiddin' me!"

"I know somebody who would say the same thing."

"Yes, I know her too."

"But as you can see Sir, I'm good and you gotta know a little somethin' somethin' about the Word in order to do that! Plus Your Honor, I talked about the Bible all the time with my sister."

"This sister being Audrey Wright, or Peaches as you call her?"

"Yep that's her. My little guy told you about her. We talked about the Bible all the time."

"You talked or did you dispute about the fact that you didn't read the Bible or live the life a Christian should live? Which one is it Mr. Addams?"

"Your Honor, I object!" James senses that he might be in a little trouble since the Judge has gone back to calling him Mr. Addams.

"You don't need to object Mr. Addams, you have the floor and you're free to talk as you please. And for the sake of clarity, to which part of the question were you objecting? Was it the 'not reading the Bible' or the 'living the life of a Christian'?"

"Well, Sir, Your Honor, it's both. We talked...we argued..." James lowers his head as he remembers his many conversations with Peaches. "...well, whatever we did, or whatever you may call it, we talked about both of them subjects all the time."

The Judge looks down at his book. "Let's switch subjects. I see here that you didn't consistently support the church you attended so faithfully with your finances. You picked and chose when you wanted to give to the ministry that appointed you to head the deacon board. Would you like to object Mr. Addams?"

"I can see you seeing it that way but let me explain something here. You see Your Honor, I was waiting for that big win, I knew it was coming and I was gon' catch up on all my tithes and offerings then. But that doggone Ellie messed that up." He starts looking around again for Ellie. "I sure hope she's somewhere up in here too, but I sure don't see her. I don't know how we got separated."

"Let's talk about you James and more importantly, let's talk about that point you brought up. I see that you played the lottery every single day, most times you played two to three times a day."

"That's true, Your Honor. I was definitely on a mission. But that's not a bad thing."

"That's called gambling."

"And…?"

"Bailiff!"

Bailiff looks down into his book. "Proverbs 28:22, '*He that rushes to be rich has an evil eye, and does not consider that poverty shall come upon him*'."

"Come on Judge, that's not fair. Everyone wants to be rich, that doesn't make them evil and poverty was already on me! Plus gambling is perfectly legal. I was not out there selling drugs, robbing banks or nothing like that. I put away all that I had for that special day to come when I won't have to struggle financially anymore. And that day came, but that got taken away as swiftly as it came."

"According to the Word, it's not God's will for your focus to be rich; in this, you lose touch with what's righteous in the eyes of the Lord. Bailiff!"

The bailiff thumbs through the pages. "Proverbs 22:16, *'He who oppresses the poor to get gain for himself, and he who gives to the rich will surely come to want'*."

James looks over at the bailiff becoming annoyed at his scripture readings. "How many times he gon' do that? And Your Honor, I don't understand what he's saying."

"James, it's wrong to bet money on the possibility of becoming instantly rich because someone is enticed to gain money by another one's loss. This is not the principle taught in the Bible. The Word tells you to work, to save, and to give. You see, lottery and other forms of gambling oppresses the poor for someone else's own personal gain. The poor people are the gambling industry and lottery institutions biggest customers."

"Wow, I didn't realize that Your Honor. You know, I never even thought about it like that. You actually may be on to something here. That makes a whole lotta sense. You need to make sure the word gets out to everyone about this. I'm so glad you told me."

"Thank you James, but now I need to ask you something. Did you ever believe that God was your source?"

"Come on Judge, I did, but I don't think this is being fair. God is the one I thought gave me that idea to get rich by playing the lottery in the first place and it seemed like a legitimate idea at the time. I deserved to have money just like the other people and that was my way. We worked hard on this plan." James turns real fast and looks at the bailiff anticipating him to read again. But the bailiff is silent. James turns back to the Judge.

The bailiff reads, "Hebrew 13:5 says '*be free from the love of money and pleased with the things which you have; for He Himself has said, I will be with you at all times*'."

The Judge motions to the bailiff. "Bailiff, please escort James to the room."

The bailiff walks over to James and begins to lead him to the room as instructed by the Judge.

James leans close to the bailiff as they approach the door and whispers so the Judge won't hear him. "Just for the record, I don't like you."

"I heard you Mr. Addams," the Judge said.

James quickly lowers his head and continues silently walking behind the smiling bailiff. They reach this huge, massive crystal glass door.

"What now, am I suppose to open it or something?" James is curious why the Judge has sent him over here. The bailiff opens the door and steps aside. When the door opens a bright light shines from inside the room blinding James. James flinches and shields his eyes from the light but continues to stand there until he can focus on what's inside this room.

Once he's able to see, he's astonished at what's inside. He tries to go into the room but there's a strange force that will not allow him to go beyond the entrance. All he can do is gaze and admire all that he sees. After a few minutes, the bailiff closes the door and leads him back to the stand.

"Wow, Your Honor, did you see that stuff in there? Of course you did, but there was wealth and riches beyond measure in that room. I saw airplanes, money for days, cars, mansions, boats, jewelry, clothes, even horses roaming about and I love horses! I mean just about everything you could possibly want in life was right there behind those doors, at least everything I've ever wanted. It even looked like there were some businesses in there. Is that the stuff you take from people who lose their cases here, or is that all your stuff?"

The bailiff reads, "Job 34:11 *'For He gives to every man the reward of his work, and sees that he gets the fruit of his ways'.*"

"What? I don't understand."

"James, let me explain. You've tried to justify your gambling habits simply because you had needs that you felt couldn't be met through your income. It was God's desire to meet your needs, every last one of them. You had a very special and specific assignment to accomplish. You were given your earthly job and your ministry at the church to bring hundreds of people to Christ.

"All those wonderful things you saw in that room, they were all yours, every last one of them. But you never received them. You never received them because you never sought God for them. Those things were to be the fruits of your labor and the rewards of your work for the Kingdom."

"Are you kiddin' me? You got to be kiddin' me! This is a joke! I know there's a punch line here…and I'm not getting it. Matter of fact, I'm not laughing." James pauses and thinks on this for a moment. "Mine… it...mine? All of that…was mine?" Jacob and LJ gasp at the thought that James was supposed to be a wealthy man.

"But wait James, there's more you did not understand," the Judge said as he motions to the bailiff.

"1Timothy 6:8-10," the bailiff reads. "*If we have food and covering, with these we shall be content. But those who want to get rich fall into temptation and a snare and many foolish and harmful desires which plunge men into ruin and destruction. For the love of money is a root of all sorts of evil, and some by longing for it have wandered away from the faith, and pierced themselves with many griefs'.*" He closes his Bible.

James stands there in disbelief. "Well, I'll be…" His disbelief now turns to anger. "Hell…that ain't my fault, Your

Honor! We need to get the people responsible for misleading me all this time! We need to get them here, right now!"

"James, only you are responsible for you. Only you can answer for you. Your sister once told you about all the things that were stored in Heaven for you. You never listened to her. You never opened up your heart."

The Judge continues to ask James more questions until He has covered all the things that need to be discussed regarding his life. "I think this is enough, let's see what The Book has for you." The Judge opens the ivory bound Book located on his desk. He turns the pages looking for James Sr.'s name. He runs his fingers up and down the columns.

"Whatcha looking for Your Honor? What book is that?"

"This is The Book of Works."

"Why you stop looking, look again. I know I'm in there. I do remember hearing the pastor talk about *The Book*. I only thought there was one book called *The Book of Life*."

"Bailiff," the Judge calls.

"Your Honor, can't you just tell me? Me and that bailiff just don't get along."

"Bailiff," He says again.

The bailiff turns to the end of the Bible. "Revelation 20:12, *'And I saw the dead, great and small, taking their places before the high seat; and The Books were open, and another book was open, which is The Book of Life; and the dead were judged by the things which were in The Books, even by their works'*."

"Well I'll be. All that's up in there? Wow." James ponders on all of this for a moment. "Your Honor, I had my faults, but I was a good man. I may not have read the Bible like I should've. I may not have tried to bring anybody into the knowledge of Jesus Christ; I may not have given to the ministry; I may not have trusted God to be my source like I should've done. I gambled, I smoked a little bit, but I was still a good man. Judge please! Considering that I did not know some of this, I believe I deserve another chance."

"I was looking for your name in The Book of Works and I can't seem to find your works anywhere in here. This book itemizes all the treasures that shall be given to you in Heaven. What you saw in the room was only your earthly treasures." The Judge closes The Book. "Bailiff."

"Hey, now back up. How can you say you can't find my works? All my life I worked. I spent a many day doing the work of the church."

"But was the work for you, for the people, for the pastor, or for God? Bailiff, please continue."

"Matthew 5:13, *'You're the salt of the earth. But if the salt loses its saltiness, how can it be made salty again? It's no longer good for anything, except to be thrown out and trampled by men'*."

"Now wait just one minute Mr. Bailiff. What you mean by good for nothing! I wish you would come over here talking about trampling somebody. If I could just get one moment with you outside this court." James takes a deep breath trying to calm himself down. "Look…I've always loved the Lord. There's got to be some explanation for this. I tell you what, just hand me that book, I know I can find it!"

"Bailiff!"

The bailiff turns the page.

James jumps in before the bailiff can read off another scripture. "Your Honor, wait, we really don't need him. Let me just find my name. I promise you, it's in there, if not that book, it must be in your other books over there."

"You're right," the Judge said. "We don't need him anymore. Enough has been said."

"No that's not what I mean Your Honor, wait! Just give me a little more time. I will prove it to you. I can do a better job, now that I know better."

The Judge motions to James. "You may return to your seat Mr. Addams. Bailiff, seat the proclaimed Christian and call the next soul."

"Wait Your Honor. I still have more to say. I can convince you that I am what I say I am."

The bailiff escorts James back to his seat, while James continues begging for another chance.

Fifteen

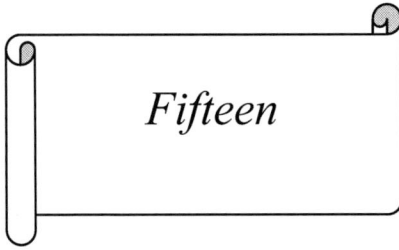

*J**ames* sits down between LJ and Jacob with his head down feeling so defeated. LJ hugs him. "It's alright dad, you did your best."

James slowly lifts up his head. "But will that be good enough, son? The question is, will it be good enough?" He lowers his head back down.

Everyone is quiet as all eyes are on James. No one knows what to do or what to expect now. Are these hearings to determine judgment or is it to determine your Christian reward? By the way things are going, it seems like the determining factor is whether any of these souls are actually Christians. Can you really get a Christian's reward, if you did not actually live the life of a Christian? So, what is a Christian? If you just believed in Jesus Christ, would you still be rewarded?

The bailiff calls another soul sitting in the courtroom, then another, and yet another. Each soul, one by one is being called to give an account of their life. They are questioned about any and everything imaginable. Some break down and cry, pleading with the Judge for another chance to do better once they realize they cannot justify their wrongdoings. Others state as James did, that they did not know. Some are happy with their hearing and some are doubtful, not really sure about this whole ordeal. Most of them think that it could go either way. No one appears to be completely sure about the outcome, even those with a good report.

The bailiff returns to the podium to call the next defendant. "Your Excellence, we call Miss Jada Jenkins to the stand."

Jada stands when she hears her name. As she starts to make her approach towards the bailiff, she becomes more confident in spite of the beating that poor James Sr. and some of the other souls have received.

The bailiff pulls out his Bible as she steps up to the stand. "Hi Miss Jenkins, do you promise to give truthful accounts of all events you will be questioned on, telling the truth and nothing but the truth?"

"Hello to you too, Sir," Jada said. "I have nothing but the truth to tell."

"Good Miss Jenkins. Are you familiar with this book?"

"Yes. I'm quite familiar with that book. It's the Bible."

"Have you read this book?"

Jada looks directly at the bailiff with the biggest smile on her face knowing from the way James' interrogation went, she got this one in the bag. "Joshua 1:8 says *'This book shall not depart from your mouth, but you shall meditate in it day and night.'* Yes sir, I've read the Bible as you can obviously tell. I've read it backwards and forwards. I've read the Bible everyday of my life since I was 17 years old. I read it when I awoke in the morning and when I retired for the night."

She looks over at James. He still looks so defeated. She's feeling a little sorry for him but there's nothing she can do so she must at least try to sell herself. Good thing she liked to read.

"Are you a Christian?"

"Yes I am. I am saved, sanctified, and filled with the Holy Spirit. I'm a born again believer and a very strong believer at that."

"Do you understand why you're here?"

"Well according to what you've said to Deacon James Addams and others, I gathered that this is the time where the people of God give an account of their lives so that we may claim our just rewards and finally come face to face with God. I would also like to say that the scripture that comes to mind right now can be found in St. John 3:3, *'Except a man be born again, he cannot see the Kingdom of Heaven'*. I'm a born again believer and I'm here to see the Kingdom of Heaven. That's what this is all about. Right?"

"Yes it is."

"But if you don't mind I would just like to say something first. Before you get all up into what you do, I would like to ask you something."

"Yes of course, you may ask."

"Thank you Mr. Bailiff. This is it. What I don't understand is why my life ended like that… so abruptly. At first, we were all sitting in here trying to figure out what was going on, and then all of a sudden, everything came back to me just as the Judge said it would. The argument, the accident, even everything before that. I can't seem to understand why it had to end the way it did. I'm sure everyone here wanted more time on earth and feel as though they left too soon. But I have an anointed voice. I could sing you right into Heaven. Don't get me wrong, I truly thank God for my gift, but I wanted to do more with that gift. I was starting to become well known and accepted in the music industry. I had so many plans for the Kingdom."

The bailiff looks up to the Judge. "Your Excellence, we have a soul proclaiming to be a Christian *who knows* the Word."

"Thank you bailiff. Miss Jada Jenkins, how do you want me to address you?"

"Oh Your Honor, it doesn't matter. Whatever you feel comfortable with."

"Thank you. I will address you as Miss Jada," the Judge says.

Jada smiles and looks over at her friends.

The Judge continues, "You're a proclaimed Christian who knows the Word?"

"That's right Your Honor, but I don't understand why the bailiff has to be so mean with me, with everyone? Why he using that *proclaiming* word on some of us and then he said *who knows the Word*? I know who I am and I know who I serve." She snaps her finger and rolls her head at the bailiff. "Thank you very much."

"Miss Jada, *proclaim* only means that you state publicly and declare that you're a follower of Jesus Christ."

"Oh, is that all that mean? Alright then, I guess it's fine. When *you* say it, it sounds so much better than when he says it."

"Miss Jada," the Judge said, "let's talk a little bit about you since I see you like talking about yourself." The Judge looks down at her and smiles. Jada smiles back at Him. "Miss Jada, I'm going to ask you some questions regarding some situations in your life. Your answers are how you will plead your case. Let's start with this one. While using your gift, how many people did you bring into the knowledge of Jesus Christ?"

"Oh Your Honor, it was too many to name. Most of the people I introduced to Christ, I've actually never dealt with them individually. The method I used to introduce people to Christ was through song. I found that once they heard me sing my message of love about the Lord, their souls were saved."

"Did you know that you cannot save souls through music? Music can enlighten you and feed your spirit, but it cannot save you. Music was created to set the atmosphere. Its purpose is to prepare the soul for worship and teaching in the spiritual realm. In the secular realm, it's designed to feed the flesh."

"Judge, you would've had to be there to see my ministry at work. I was really good. You could ask anyone, Jacob, James, even LJ. They will tell you how good I was." LJ is in the back shaking his head agreeing with Sister Jada.

"Bailiff," the Judge said.

"Yes Your Honor," the bailiff said as he opened his Bible. "According to James 1:17, '*Every good gift and every perfect gift is from above*'."

"And yes, I agree with that, you're preaching to the choir little man, and I mean that literally," Jada said. "I acknowledge that God gave this gift to me. He gave it to me to use for His Kingdom. It was my job to sing, so I sang. Through my singing, people were being ministered to."

"So, what you are saying, is that you personally never took the time out to minister to lost souls one-on-one, other than through singing. "

"Well not exactly Your Honor, I had my group of friends and associates that I talked to. It's just that singing was my passion and my ministry. It was my method to reach the masses. I didn't have a lot of time for any one-on-one, personal stuff. I talked about the Word to those who asked...but I can't say for sure if any of them became saved. But you know, as I think about it that should count because I did talk to them. I was so busy and committed to my ministry. My schedule became very grueling through the latter part of my life."

"Grueling for whom?"

"For the Kingdom of God, of course," Jada said.

"And if I may ask you this question, what souls were you reaching at the Wild Card?"

"Now Your Honor, that was a little different. That was my way of becoming established in the business so I could eventually be able to reach more souls. The people in the world needed to be reached so that was how I planned to reach them. In that, I had a following in the secular and Gospel realm. You have to admit that was a really good plan, plus those people who came to see me at the club became very close to me. We established a tight relationship which would've eventually opened up their hearts to me so they could hear the Word. And it would've worked, but I left too soon which is what I really need to find out about. What was up with that, if you don't mind me asking Sir, I mean Your Honor?"

"Bailiff!"

The bailiff stands and starts to search through the scriptures.

"Heyyyyy! There couldn't possibly be a scripture for that situation! I really didn't say anything!"

"Bailiff, go ahead."

"2Corinthians 6:14," the Bailiff reads. "*Be not unequally or unfairly bonded together with unbelievers; for what friendship has righteousness with unrighteousness? And what spiritual union have light with darkness*?" He closes the Bible.

"See, like I said there's not a scripture for that. You know that was not a good example. Did I say anything about marrying them? That was not appropriate for this situation."

"You see Miss Jada, that's where most people have made their mistakes with the Word, the Judge said "Since that scripture is almost always used for a particular situation people tend to believe it only applies to that. They also tend not to read the entire scripture. You can't stop at what suits you, you must read its entire passage and get its full meaning. Being unfairly bonded or unequally yoked with an unbeliever as you know, it's not just based on marriage. Yes it deals with relationships, but all relationships are not about marriage. You as a *proclaimed* Christian can't live according to the rules of the world and still maintain your sanctification. God called you to be sanctified. When you're sanctified, you move away, set yourself apart, become cleansed from the ways of the world. Either you are for God or you are against God. You cannot be both. Let's go to something else."

"If I must say Your Honor, and you did say that we could speak freely." Before she continues, she looks up at the Judge and waits for His response. The Judge nods. "Okay then, I still don't think that was a good example."

"Would you like another one Miss Jada, one that you might feel more comfortable with?"

"Well…"

"Bailiff, help Miss Jada out, please. Don't be so confusing this time, causing her to have to think about it. With this scripture, I want you to get directly to the point and hit the nail on the head. Can you do that for me?"

The bailiff opens the Bible and turns the pages in search of something else. "Oh, here's a good one, Your Honor. You will be pleased. Romans 12:2, *'Do not obey, copy, imitate the behavior, rules, or customs of this world; but be changed'*, or should I say, *'transformed by the renewing of your mind'*…" He looks up from the Bible at Jada. "Is that it or should I continue?"

Jada folds her arms across her chest, "I think you've said enough!"

"Oh no," the Judge said. "You haven't even finished that one verse. At least finish the entire verse!"

He continues. *"Then you will learn to know God's will for you, which is good and pleasing and perfect."*

"Alright, alright, I know the verse. I know it very well. You've made your point."

"Are you sure, Miss Jada? Shall I go on to the next subject?" the Judge asked.

The big smile Jada had at the beginning is slowly fading away. She hesitates. "Yes Sir… I guess so." *I was a good Christian, I was a good Christian*—she keeps repeating to herself. *This is only a trial and I can prove my case because I've been such an asset to the Kingdom of God.* Jada continues to talk to herself, hoping this will help build herself up.

"Alright Miss Jada, am I correct in saying that while you were working at the Wild Card you began to drink alcohol?" He leafs through the pages in The Book. "Ummmmmm, I would say quite frequently."

"Yes, but I was never intoxicated. I began drinking wine to clear my head. I'm not gon' lie, sometimes I even had some of the strong stuff, but most of the time, it was wine. Look Your Honor; there's a lot of stress and pressure when you have a gift like mine. But it was never said in the Word that we couldn't drink alcohol, it just said in 1st Corinthians that drunkards, and let me emphasize *drunkards*, won't inherit the Kingdom of God. Look at me, I am not a drunkard. Three or four drinks do not constitute drunkenness."

Jada quickly looks over to the bailiff and stares him down because she knows he cannot quote a scripture that can refute the one she just quoted for herself. The bailiff does not move or respond to Jada's stares.

"Bailiff!" the Judge said.

Jada starts stomping her feet having a mini-tantrum on the stand. She can't believe what's happening. "Come on Your Honor, I know I'm right on this one!"

The bailiff smiles and thumbs through the pages of the Bible. "Okay, Galatians 5:13, *'you have been called to live in liberty, in freedom, to serve one another in love. But don't use that freedom to satisfy the flesh, your sinful nature.'*"

Jada gives the bailiff a puzzled look. She turns to address the Judge. "See Your Honor, I could do his job! He does not know how to rightly divide the Word of God! Now what does that have to do with drinking?"

"Miss Jada, let me paint a picture for you. Let's say that Christians are free to drink, or let's even say to drink in moderation as long as they do not become *intoxicated*. But ask yourself this question. Is that what you *should* do as a Christian? Ponder on this thought for a moment. How can you be filled with the Holy Spirit *and* alcohol, which is a mind altering drug, at the same time? What form of glory does God get from your drinking?"

The bailiff looks up at the Judge, "May I, your—".

"Why don't you just shut up? It's obvious I can lose this case all by myself. I really don't need your help." Jada yells.

The Judge looks at Jada. "You believe you've lost your case?"

"The bailiff is making me look bad!"

"Is he really, Miss Jada? Have you any faith, even in yourself?"

"I've plenty of faith in me, it's just others I have a problem with."

The Judge turns to the bailiff. "Go on."

"Galatians 6:8, *'for he that sows to his flesh shall of the flesh reap corruption, but he that sows to the Spirit shall of the Spirit reap everlasting life.'*"

"Come on Your Honor, this is not fair. That has absolutely nothing to do with drinking. Now there are some scriptures about wine and strong drink and he ain't even using them! I think the bailiff has been drinking and smoking something."

"So you admit that drinking and smoking can have an adverse affect on you, even a spirit?"

"Only in his case!"

"Well Miss Jada, anything you do to your body, especially if you know that it's harmful, is a sin. Drinking and smoking over a period of time causes much damage to the body, the temple that houses your spirit. Your flesh becomes addicted and desires that nicotine, that drug and alcohol more and more. In this you're sowing to or satisfying your flesh. Your spirit on the other hand, will never desire those things. Anything that's addictive is not of God. Only the things of God can feed your spirit."

"Your Honor, I don't get it. How can you find so much wrong with all the good things I've done? You haven't once mentioned any of the good stuff. I read my Bible every single day no matter what; I prayed, I fellowshipped with believers, I fed the hungry and gave to many unfortunate people.

"Yes, I admit I've made mistakes from time to time, but we all sin, every last soul in here has sinned. Even the bailiff here has sinned, I can tell. But my heart was pure, Your Honor. So please, tell me all that I've done has mattered. Tell me that you will be merciful and will judge me according to my deeds, my works, the activities I performed in and for the body of Christ."

"Jada, you did do all those things, you did some wonderful things for the *sake* of the Kingdom. But you're not justified through your works, only through your faith and through grace. You had many works, but what about your faith?"

"But Your Honor—"

"Bailiff!"

"Not again," Jada said. She's so tired of the bailiff quoting scriptures. It's reminding her of her last conversations with her ex-best friend, Maxine.

The bailiff clears his throat but does not open the Bible. "Righteousness comes through confidence in Jesus Christ to all who believe in Him. For every one *has* sinned, as you've said, and fallen short of God's glory. You are freely acceptable by God's grace through the liberation that came by Christ Jesus."

"Now is that supposed to be some ad lib or did you think of that all by yourself? I thought you were going to say *'faith without works is dead'*," Jada said with her hands on her hips and working her neck at the same time.

"I'm not against you Miss Jada," the bailiff said. "I gave you an analogy of scripture to help you see inside yourself, and it also goes along with what you are pleading for yourself."

"I don't see where you're helping me at all. Every scripture you give only makes me look more guilty."

"Miss Jada," the Judge said. "You claimed to know God's Word from front to back, so you should know that no one will be declared righteous in God's sight just by doing what's considered right in the law. The purpose of the law was to make you conscious of sin. You must have faith."

The Judge continues, "I want to establish some things here. From your own admission, you smoked, drank, and participated in worldly parties, which you called work. As I look in The Book, it also tells me that you lied, had an arrogant spirit, and…look at this one. You had a continuous sexual relationship outside of marriage."

James whispered over to Jacob, "Oh, she gon' get it now. But you know that girl can talk herself out of anything." Jacob nods.

Jada frowns at this obvious case against her. "Your Honor, that should not be held against me. Yes, it's true, I did fornicate, but we were going to get married. We loved each other very much; you already know what type of guy he is. But I don't understand why you think I lied or was proud or arrogant. I can't say that I never lied, but not intentionally, at least that I remember. And arrogance, I think you're misunderstanding my confidence. I was a very self-confident person."

"Alright. So let's go over those points you've made. You fornicated with the person you were planning to marry; which happened to be the person you ran from, which ultimately resulted in your death and the death of others. At some time in that relationship I can assess that he asked for your hand in marriage and you accepted"

Jada does not respond. She lowers her head in shame because she knows she cannot justify her actions with Aaron. She knows she was wrong and she knows that she initiated it.

The best way to answer this one is to not answer. So Jada does not respond to the Judge.

"That's fine. You don't have to answer that one. Bailiff!"

"2Corinthians 6:14," the bailiff reads. *"Be ye not unequally yoked together with unbelievers—"*

Jada jumps up and down in frustration, "That does it! I've had it with him! This is so unfair. Now he used that one already. And the bad thing about it is, this is actually the right time to use it." Jada thinks about what she has just said. "Oops," she places her hands over her mouth and puts her head back down.

"Shall I finish it Your Honor?" The bailiff looks up to the Judge.

"No bailiff, from Miss Jada's reaction, I think she understands the meaning quite well." He looks down at her. "Would you like to take this opportunity to explain?"

Jada takes a deep breath. "Yes, I would Your Honor." She knows she's in trouble for this one but she just might be able to pull this one off once He hears her side. "I met Aaron at the club at my very first performance and we hit it off so well. It was like everything was perfect between us. This man was so kind, loving and giving. He became my protector, my provider, my confidant, and my best friend when everyone else I loved turned their back on me.

"Even though he was not in the church originally, I knew I could win him over because his heart was pure like mine. Yes, we became romantically, intimately involved before he became saved and most importantly before we were married. But it was me who brought him into the knowledge of Christ. No matter what the circumstances are, some things are just meant to be, and Aaron and I was that." Jada points at LJ. "Your Honor, remember what he did for LJ at the accident scene. When you talked with LJ you said Aaron is now teaching the Gospel which such zeal; truly I had something to do with that. It was me who gave him that foundation."

"Miss Jada, you had a lot to do with him teaching the Word. A lot of his motivation was based on the last day of your and LJ's lives. I want you to reflect on your final conversation with him."

Jada thinks back on her last moments with Aaron. The fight was so intense. He was only telling her what was right and she didn't want to hear it. All she could think about was herself and her own desires. Not once did she consider what turmoil he might've been going through. Not once did she even think about allowing him the time to grow and be nurtured in the Word of God. Jada just felt like she was being deserted once again by someone she loved.

Yes, she had a major role in Aaron's ministry, but it was appearing as if her selfish actions may have become his inspirational message. She too is starting to feel defeated, just like James. This is not what she expected.

"Miss Jada…, are you with us?" The Judge looks down towards her.

"I'm sorry, Your Honor, I apologize. I was just thinking about something." Jada's voice is so soft; her words are almost a whisper.

"Are you okay Miss Jada?"

"No I am not Your Honor."

"I'm sorry but I must continue."

"You mean there's more?"

"We've not really addressed the lies and pride issues."

"Lies and pride issues? I don't have those kinds of issues!"

"Did you cheat on your taxes?"

Jada pauses before answering this question. She knows she must say the right things to make up for some of the things she couldn't explain away. "Well, yes, but everybody does that. Cheating on your taxes is a given. Actually, it's not really cheating because you're only taking back the money the government took from you without asking. It's an established practice to get as much of your own money back as possible."

"So cheating is not cheating if it's done for the right reason?"

"Correct…uhhh; no…I'm so confused."

"Cheating is just a combination of two sins, stealing and lying. Bailiff!"

"The Word reads in Mark 10:19, '*don't murder, don't commit adultery, don't steal or give false testimony, don't defraud*' or should we say cheat, '*honor your mother and father*.'" He closes the Bible and sits down.

"This is not good," Jada says as she looks around the room at all the souls looking directly back at her. She now realizes what some of them felt. It appears as if the Judge is throwing one question after another at her and it's not looking as good as she thought her life looked.

"Did you tell people when they answered your phone to say you were not home when you were?" the Judge asks.

She puts her head down again. She never even thought twice about that one. It has now reached the point where she does not even know whether or not she should speak. No matter what she says it seems as if the deck is stacked against her and she just can't understand how all this happened. She looks up at the Judge and speaks softly. "Yes...but..." She begins to play with her hands, not knowing what else to do.

"Did you believe *you* were the reason people responded to the Lord when you sang?"

She holds her head up in excitement. Finally, redemption! This is her opportunity to shine. She can definitely sell herself on her singing, maybe she wasn't totally defeated after all.

"Yes Your Honor, I did. Let me sing a song for you so you can understand what I've been trying to tell you." Jada clears her throat, and then opens her mouth to sing. Nothing comes out. She tries again but the same thing happens. Jada starts to panic and keeps trying. "Oh my God, Your Honor, something is wrong. My voice! It's gone!"

"Nothing is wrong Miss Jada. Here you have no need of the gifts that you were given here. The purpose of your gift was to use on earth to draw men and use it for the glory of God. The gift was yours to enjoy and to minister to others. You are no longer on earth and there's no one here for you to minister to, so there's no further need for your gift here at this time. You still possess it, you just cannot use it in this place."

"But I need to show you how good I am. How else can I prove my case? If you can just find a way to get it back, just once more…I promise you, you will understand."

"Proof comes from the life that you lived, the life you are here defending. Let me explain about your talent, your gift from God. Music is not salvation. It does not save a single soul. As I said earlier, music is supposed to create an atmosphere for worship but we know when satan gets involved it's just the opposite. Gospel music creates an atmosphere for the people to be open to the Word.

"When you sang, you allowed them to recognize and be open to their pain and their joy so that they may receive and acknowledge Christ. Secular music on the other hand created an atmosphere that placed the minds of people on the works of satan. There's no glory for God with secular music because its purpose is not intended to glorify Him."

"I really didn't know that."

"That's because you didn't seek a true relationship with your Heavenly Father. What you did was become religious and ritualistic. You had the foundation to establish that relationship but you pulled back and did what you thought would make you look elevated in the eyes of man. Once you truly develop a relationship with God, everything you do is all about Him."

Jada once again puts her head down but this time tears are falling down her cheeks. "But there were some things that I did right. Right? You said so earlier."

"The point is Jada, which you and the bailiff pointed out already, every man sins almost every single day of his life. I know that because you were made more flesh than spirit. That's why Jesus had to come after the fall of the first man, Adam. You needed an example of true righteousness and Jesus became that, because no other man was capable. But even in that exemplary life, Jesus had to feel and experience every pain and temptation that you would possibly have to feel and experience.

"Jesus' purpose was to prove God's love for you by giving you another chance, and another chance and another chance.

And even though you are given many chances, Jesus still speaks, fights, and intercedes on your behalf. But the only thing that matters now is, did you ever take the time to repent of your sins when you were doing that which you knew was unrighteous in the eyes of the Lord?"

"I really don't know, Sir. I think I did. But most of the time, I believed I was righteous, so why should I repent?"

"Even those who consider themselves righteous in the eyes of the Lord, must still repent and that's because of your flesh. The only way to never repent would be if you never sin, and you've already stated that each and every soul in here sins each and every day. I'm sorry Miss Jada, but that's enough, I think we've covered everything. Let's see where you stand."

"I understand Your Honor. I also believe everything's gon' be alright." Jada takes a deep breath.

He takes out the ivory bound Book and flips the pages looking for Jada's name. He runs his fingers up and down the columns. "I'm afraid I don't see it."

Jada turns toward the Judge shocked at his answer. "Surely Judge, you saw my name. You had to see it! Maybe you're not spelling it right. That's J-A-D-A."

"I know the spelling and your name is not here with all the good you did. With all your reading, praying, singing, worshipping, and giving of your time and possessions, you never once repented in your heart of your sins so it was not recorded. You may be seated. Bailiff!"

"Wait Your Excellence, what do you mean not recorded? How can I repent for wrong I was not aware of? I did what I thought was right to me."

"Ignorance is no excuse. And ignorance was not your problem. You had access to the truth. The truth was told to you constantly through your church, family and friends. You even spoke and sang the truth with your own mouth, but never with your heart. Your problem was, you wanted the best of both worlds." He nods to the bailiff.

"Proverbs 14:12 *'There is a way that seems right to a man, but in the end it leads to death'*."

"Death! What do you mean death?"

"Miss Jada," the Judge said. "Please be seated."

"You're condemning me. No, this can't be. This cannot be your last words to me. You've completely misjudged me. I'm not that bad. I helped the church, I helped all my friends. I was the one who made a difference. I helped everyone. If it wasn't for me...I...." Jada stops in the middle of her sentence and begins to cry. She realizes how selfish and proud she had been all along. Jada steps down from the stand and slowly walks back to her seat.

Sixteen

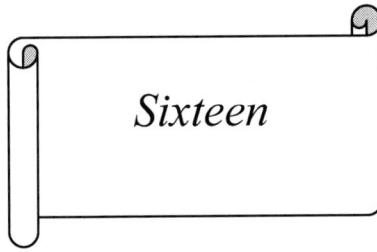

*T*he bailiff returns to the front of the podium to call the next soul. "Your Excellence, I call Jacob Wright to the stand.

Jacob rises. As he approaches Jada, he tries to hug her but she does not respond. Jacob decides to just hold her anyway. Jada cries deeply on his shoulder. Jacob looks up and addresses the Judge. "I'm sorry Your Honor, I'm not trying to be disrespectful, I'm coming. This was hard on her and I thought Sister Jada could use some compassion right now." The Judge smiles and nods in agreement and motions to the bailiff to allow it. After a moment or two, Jada begins to compose herself. Jacob helps Jada to her seat, walks to the front of the courtroom and approaches the bailiff. The bailiff pulls out his Bible to begin the proceedings with Jacob.

"Hi Mr. Jacob Wright. Do you promise to give truthful accounts of all events you will be questioned on, telling the truth and nothing but the truth?"

"Yes Sir."

"Are you familiar with this book?"

"Yes Sir, I am." He glances over the bailiff's shoulder to see if Jada is alright. He knows deep inside that it's probably not, especially after that interrogation. But he's concerned about her and his uncle anyway. Jada waves her hand to him to let him know to go on and not to bother with her, what's done is done. James also gives him a nod.

"Did you read its contents?"

"As much as I could. I've read and studied but never in its entirety. And I'm sure there was so much more for me to learn, but I guess my time ran out. I did my best," he looks up at the Judge. "I hope." He looks back and forth from the bailiff to the Judge hoping to catch some type of positive emotion.

"Do you understand why you're here?"

"Yes…but…no, actually I'm confused. I was so sure that there was so much more for me to do. I wanted to help so many people. I thought I had a mission in life. Did I miss what God was saying to me?"

"The Judge will explain everything to you." The bailiff places the Bible down on the small stand and stands before the Judge. "Your Excellence, I present to you a *proclaimed* Christian."

The Judge looks down at His list. He immediately picks up the large ivory bound Book without questioning Jacob at all.

This is completely unlike what He did with the others that came before Him. The Judge looks over the contents of The Book and rubs His chin. "Jacob, before I go on with any of the events in your life, let's first clear up any questions you may have."

"Thank you because I do have a question. It's like this Your Honor; I thought I was called in the ministry to teach others about God's love, especially to the young and the hurt, because I could relate to them. I fought being in the ministry for a long time but I could tell that God was working something in me. I needed to go through what I went through for a greater good. The only thing was I just didn't know how or when God was going to use me."

"That's very true Jacob. You had a big assignment."

"If that's true, then why did I not get the chance to minister, to win people over to Christ? I know I could've done so much to help our church and community, even at school. People were thirsty for the Word and didn't even know it. I could've brought so many souls to Christ, even my brother, not that he wasn't saved. My brother was a good guy, but he was struggling with his flesh. He was always ready to react, no matter what the cost. I know I could've reached him, I just needed more time with him. But then not only him, I just wanted everyone to know and feel what I felt about the Lord."

"Jacob, you did minister to your brother, to your friends and everyone you came in contact with; and you did it to the very end. Ministry is not always standing behind a pulpit preaching to a room of people. Ministry is just a method of sharing the message of salvation and it can come in many forms. You reached people in ways you never would have imagined." He turns to the bailiff. "Bailiff! Turn on the screen. Jacob, pay close attention."

The bailiff moves over to the side of the courtroom where a giant projection-like screen sits in the corner. He snaps his finger. All the lights in the room go off and the screen immediately comes to life.

✠

Joshua is in the pulpit preaching hard for the people to repent while there's time. He's telling them to give God this day because tomorrow may not come, for no day is promised.

Joshua ends his sermon and begins his altar call, calling people to give their lives to Jesus. A dark burly figure slowly makes his way down the aisle with his head down. Joshua notices him coming down the aisle and freezes. The man walks directly up to him and stops. Joshua is unable to speak.

"I know you may not understand me or even be able to help me," the man says. "But I've come to you to say I'm sorry.

I've already asked God to forgive me. But I had to come to you as well. I hope that you too can find a spot in your heart for forgiveness."

Joshua continues to stand there completely motionless. When Peaches notices Joshua's strange behavior, she leaves the choir stand and walks up to both of them. She places her hand on Joshua's shoulder.

"Joshua!" She nudges him on the shoulder. "Joshua, are you alright?"

Joshua is still unable to speak and does not respond to his mother. He's still looking at the man who has just approached him in the church.

The burly man turns to Peaches. "I owe you an apology as well, Mrs. Wright. Even though I was not the one who pulled the trigger on the gun that ended Jacob's life..."

Peaches gasps at this acknowledgment of her son's murder and places her hand over her mouth.

"...I however hold myself just as responsible. I've had to pay for that horrible day and I've paid dearly, but not nearly as much as you. But please, listen to me. At that moment, just before his life was taken, I wanted to commit myself back to God; I just didn't know how to respond. The words he said to me have echoed in my head every single day and every single night of my life since that horrible day. He said to me, 'you will be a new creature and all this you're doing won't be important to you any more. And what's even better, God won't hold it against you, you will be completely forgiven! Who cares what man thinks, it only matters what God does'…"

Tears are flowing heavily down the cheeks of Antonio 'Tiny' Dixon as he reiterates the words of Jacob who has been a part of his thoughts since his death. His actions toward Joshua and Jacob were his personal lashing out on the church, based on his own hurt from how the church of his past had treated him and his parents.

Elder Cornell and Christian Dixon, made a hasty financial decision without the approval of their church board due to the deadline of the project. One of the board members who was also a deacon of the church, was incensed by this decision. He was envious even more of the loyal following the couple had worked so hard to cultivate.

The deacon's sister was a columnist for a large newspaper so he gave her information that this *larger-than-life* minister was stealing funds from the people of the churches and organizations which he led. In her column, she reported a possible scandal in the church, which led to a major investigation into the church and his father's financial accounts. It turned out the bookkeeping had been doctored. He was found guilty of tax fraud and misappropriation of funds. He was also fined one hundred thousand dollars and sentenced to serve five years at a minimum security prison. Elder Cornell

Dixon was made an example and a warning to other church leaders that they were not above the law.

Tiny and his mother was ousted from the church, from their home, with no money and no where to go. Their accounts had been frozen. His father died a few months into serving his sentence from a massive heart attack. This happened while attending a service at the prison ministry he started there.

The guilt of the deacon became so heavy. He just thought the elder would be ostracized from the church. He never expected all this to happen, so he came forth a couple of months after the death of Elder Dixon and admitted he had lied and forged the books. His sister was fired from her job at the newspaper and the deacon was tried and sentenced to the same facility where Elder Dixon had served. But this hadn't changed anything for Tiny and his mom, the real damage had already been done.

All the people at Holy Tabernacle Church stood silently listening and watching Minister Joshua Wright and Tiny. A few of the Armor Bearers and some members of The God Squad, moved alongside the minister, not knowing what to expect from this visitor. Joshua raised his hand, letting them know, to stop and stand still right where they were. Pastor Devine came and stood right next to his Minister of Music, Audrey 'Peaches' Wright.

One of the ushers walks up behind Tiny and hands him a tissue to wipe his tear-stained face. He dabs at his eyes and tries to compose himself so that he may continue to talk to Peaches, to Joshua, to the entire congregation.

"…I will, of course, understand if none of you here can bring yourselves to forgive me for playin' a role in taking away such a strong and wonderful man of God. I just needed you to know that I'm saved now and it's all because of Jacob, your son, your brother, your friend, your member. I've been struggling with coming here and the Holy Spirit led me here because now was the time. Joshua, when I walked in and heard you preaching, I could actually hear Jacob. I'm sure you would've made your little brother proud." Tiny turns around and begins to exit down the aisle.

Joshua yells out to him. *"Tiny! Stop right there! You will not get the chance to run away this time!"*

Tiny stops immediately and turns around to face Joshua. He knew this was a long time coming and he was prepared to face whatever Joshua felt was necessary, to deal with the loss of his brother. He knew his influence led to the death of his brother, Jacob.

Joshua walks down the aisle and stops directly in front of Tiny, facing the man who was just as much responsible for the murder of his brother as the man who pulled the trigger.

Peaches continues to stand there holding Pastor Devine's hand. She does not yet know what to do or even what Joshua will do.

Joshua stares him in the face.

"Tiny, let me tell you something and this has been a long time coming. My brother Jacob once said to me, 'fist for fist is not always the answer to everything'. He said sometimes you just got to hit your knees. And he was right. Because of the light that was in him that he has spiritually passed on to me, I can easily say...I forgive you my brother. Welcome...to the family...and the body of Christ." Joshua reaches out and Tiny literally falls into his open arms. Both of them stand there, hugging and crying together. Peaches runs down the aisle and joins the embrace. The congregation crowds around them as they all begin to sing, cry, hug, and worship as one.

⌗

The screen goes blank and immediately, the lights come on at the snap of the bailiff's finger. James, Jada, LJ, and of course, Jacob are all crying.

"Bailiff," the Judge calls out.

"Matthew 5:16 says, *'Let your light so shine before men, that they may see your good works and glorify your Father which is in Heaven'.*"

"You see, Jacob," the Judge speaks. "Your job was to plant the seed. You were only supposed to live your life so that others may see God in you. Your life assignment was to be the example, to be as much like Jesus as humanly possible. It was never your job to do the watering and nurturing of the Word; just the planting.

"You were on earth to prove to certain people that holiness could be achieved at your age. You were not perfect, but you knew when to repent for your faults, your sins. Because of your life and your death, Joshua became the man he was supposed to be in God; to carry out the purpose or life assignment that you actually thought was yours. Because of your life and your death, Tiny turned his whole life around and came back to Christ where he belonged. God never stopped loving him. He's now the Champlain of the prison ministry where some of his old gang members are serving time. Your life assignment has been fulfilled."

Jacob continues to wipe the tears from his eyes and looks up to the Judge. "But, what about my mom? I know she has suffered so much with this. Losing my dad a few months earlier, and then all of us here around the same time. This had to be enough to drive her over the edge. She was a powerful woman of God, but this had to be too much. She didn't deserve all that grief and pain."

"Jesus was handed over to die. He was severely beaten and tortured and unjustly killed. Do you know of anyone who could've endured what He endured? This was done to Him because of sin by you, by Peaches, and by everyone else who was born and to be born. But then He was raised to life to make you and everyone else right with God. So, did Jesus deserve all that grief and pain?"

The Judge looks at Jacob. Jacob nods in agreement of the point the Judge has made. "Yes Jacob, your mom suffered tremendous losses. And unfortunately, good people suffer all the time as was the case with your cousin, LJ. Yes, she's also a powerful woman of God, obediently at work in the ministry. And yes, throughout all the suffering from that ordeal, she suffered the most. Your pain was for just a moment. She lost her husband... her friend... her brother... her nephew... and of course you... her son, all in one year. She even lost Joshua for a short period of time after your death. He became consumed with your death and his inability to forgive himself. He believed everything that happened was his fault. But eventually, he too came around.

But God had an enormous amount of grace, mercy and compassion for the Wright family. You see the story didn't end as it did on the screen. There was more. All of the lottery tickets purchased by the Addams family was found inside the wreckage and all the contents of the car was given to the only survivor of that accident… Ellie Addams."

James slowly rises, in shock at the mention of Ellie. It had never occurred to him that there might've been a survivor of the crash.

"…However, since Ellie was badly injured in the accident becoming a quadriplegic, totally incapable of handling financial affairs, your mom, Audrey was named executor of the Addams estate. She set up a foundation that would take care of Ellie for the rest of her life. She has seen to it that Ellie will always be as comfortable as her condition allows. She also, through Ellie's permission and insistence, draws a salary from the account which she in turn, uses a substantial amount of the money to finance the works of the ministry.

"Ever since Tiny visited them at the church, she has funded his prison ministry and works hand-in-hand with him and the inmates as well, even the one who actually pulled the trigger and killed her son. You see Jacob, what satan means for bad, God will turn it all around for good, if you're truly one of His own."

James sits back down. He's more ashamed than ever of his earlier comments of his wife Ellie, hoping she was there with them.

How could I have been so callous all these years? he wondered. *I loved my wife but did I ever really show her? Did I ever make her feel loved, truly loved? She was so perfect and we were so happy. She always did whatever I told her to do and I liked that about her. But eventually, I just took over her whole personality.*

LJ looks up at his father, concerned about him.

Oh my God, he continued to think. *What have I done? I took Ellie for granted. I led my family astray. I didn't mean it, but I did. I knew the Word, I just liked my way better; it was easier, so I thought. Good thing my sister was such a strong woman and was able to influence LJ in the right way.*

Jacob notices LJ looking up at his father and becomes concerned about the look on his face. He wonders whether he should go to him, but decides to stay there.

James' countenance slightly changes as he thinks a little more about his wife. Well good for you Ellie, even though you may not be able to walk. You are alive. This will be your chance to get right and do right by not being negatively influenced by people like me. You deserve a second chance and thank you God...thank you God, for giving it to her. Thank you God so very much.

James Sr. holds his head up for the first time since he was on the stand. He sits proud with a smile on his face, a smile of comfort believing that regardless of what happens to him, Ellie will be alright. Jada places her arm around him as LJ holds his hand.

✠

Jacob was pleased with the Judge's account of what happened with his mother. "Thank you Your Excellence ...for everything. I now understand that You had the bigger picture in mind while I could only see what was in front of me."

"You are welcome, Jacob. If there are no more questions from you, I also have nothing further. You may be seated." He closes The Book and looks over at James Sr. as Jacob is stepping down from the stand.

"James Addams Sr." He calls out. James stands up immediately as LJ holds his hand.

"Yes Sir, Your Honor."

"I just wanted you to know... you're welcome."

LJ looks up at his father not understanding. James on the other hand is amazed and happy all at the same time at the Judge's statement. Was he thinking out loud? Of course not. The Judge knew his thoughts. If the Judge is who he thinks He's and His comment is what he thinks it means, then he knows that Ellie will be fine. No thanks to him, but nonetheless, she will be alright. He smiles and nods to the Judge. James sits down and hugs his son tightly as the bailiff escorts Jacob back to his seat. They all lovingly hug each other.

Seventeen

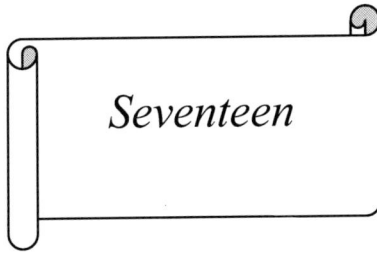

*T*he souls sit somberly in the courtroom not really knowing what to do or expect next. They had come before the Judge and presented their case, their life. Some were good, some were bad, but they all explained their behavior and decisions. The Judge was rough yet compassionate in His questioning. He covered quite a few things in their lives. There were some really terrible things the souls mentioned to the Judge. They all wanted to let Him know how they changed for the better, compared to where they started. He would tell them that He did not see any of it written in the enormous books He had on His desk. The Judge would just say, "Let's go on". It kind of discouraged some of them because they based their entire case on those bad times in their lives which they repented for. Whether or not they felt the Judge had good records, they did feel as if they still had a pretty good chance to make it to the next level.

The Judge nods and the bailiff approaches the front of the courtroom. He looks around at all the souls. His expression shows neither acceptance or rejection. He notices the tension in their faces. The bailiff knows his job of quoting The Word is hard on the souls. However, his main objective is simply to enlighten them to the fact that God placed all the answers to life in the Bible. They only had to take the time to search and place the answers in their hearts. God really loved these humans. His heart was so big and even more so, He was so forgiving of their mistakes just as long as they asked for it and meant it.

The bailiff takes a deep breath and begins to speak. "The righteous cried out and the Lord, my God, heard you and delivered you out of all your troubles. The Lord was near when you had a broken heart and saved you who had a repentant spirit. Many were the afflictions of the righteous, but the Lord delivered you out of them all. Though you fell, He didn't utterly cast you down. He upheld you. He hid His face from your sins and blotted out all your transgressions, because of your repentant spirit. There's not a soul amongst you that always did what was right. Some of your ways may have been right in your own eyes, so God did not judge your ways, He judged your heart. It was the heart that revealed the truth. Therefore, trying to be righteous and just was more acceptable to Him than your sacrifices. God knew who really represented Him."

The bailiff pauses, looks back to the Judge who's watching him, and takes another deep breath. He turns back to face the souls.

"For all of you, a child was born, God's greatest of all gifts to you. And unto Him a Son was given. As for now, all has been heard and here's the conclusion of the matter regarding your lives. Your purpose for life on earth was to revere God and keep *His* laws. In keeping His laws, you would learn to love and help one another.

"In doing this, you would not have time to just focus on your own desires. God never even encouraged you to fulfill all of your desires. Part of your mission included controlling some of your desires. So now, God has brought every obvious and hidden deed into judgment, whether it was good or evil. Judgment...has now begun...with the people of God."

The Judge immediately strikes the gavel as the bailiff ends his speech and returns to his seat. All of the souls' eyes are on the Judge, realizing the magnitude of the bailiff's words.

A tall ominous figure, who had gone completely unnoticed, was sitting in the back corner of the courtroom. He gets up and slowly walks towards the front. Everyone turns to look at him as he walks past their row where he occasionally stops and looks at them. He continues his slow stroll to the front, making sure they can all see him.

In the meantime, the Judge continues with his summation to the souls:

"I'm sure by now you all understand and know who I am. *I AM THAT I AM.* You're here because there's one thing all of you have in common. This room is filled with souls that have acknowledged the true existence of the Father, the Son, and the Holy Spirit. You're all the ones who proclaim yourselves as a Christian; whether you called yourselves, Baptist, Pentecostal, Catholic, Jehovah's Witness, Apostolic, etc.

"As a Christian, not a denomination, but as a Christian, you were the most powerful people on earth and some of you didn't even realize it. You had the knowledge of true salvation and access to My Word which entitled you to a source of untapped power. Many before you and even some of you, have died for that access, that power, that knowledge of salvation through Jesus Christ. Salvation was a gift and it was freely given to each and every one of you. The only One, who had to pay the price for it, was Jesus, My Beloved Son.

"In your Christian life, you had three levels to achieve. The first level; being saved, was actually your easiest. It only required you to believe in your heart that Jesus is Lord and to confess and proclaim the miracle of His birth, life, death, and resurrection. I must commend you. All of you have made it to that level or you would not be here. You would be in the other courtroom, and believe me; you do not want to be in there." The souls look around at each other.

"The second level you needed to achieve was to learn all about Me. I placed everything you needed to know in My Manual, which you know as the Bible. How can you effectively worship and be committed to someone or even something that you know nothing about? To hear about, only peaks your interest. To learn about, gives you knowledge, which brings power. You then can tell others and build a relationship, because you know for yourself. This is where your faith strengthens because you learn that you can do all things through Jesus who is the One who strengthens you.

"The third level was the real test. I like to call it *The Walk of Salvation*. Not only did you have to believe, learn and talk the Word, but you had to walk it. It was made simple in 1John 2:6, 'Whoever claims to live in Me must walk as Jesus did.' Becoming saved was important because you could never achieve the other levels without having salvation. But learning, talking, and walking in the Word was your ultimate path to eternal life. Some of you allowed the things of this world to influence you and eventually become your god.

"Paul warned you in Romans 7:19, 'Nothing good lives in you; that is, in your sinful nature. You desire to do good, but cannot carry it out. For what you do is not the good you want to do. The evil you don't want to do is what you keep on doing. Now if you do what you don't want to do, it's no longer you who does it, but it's sin living in you that does the wrong.'

"What I had Paul tell you was this, there's absolutely no good thing in the flesh that once held your souls. Every time you tried to do right, wrong would rise up in you, from the very sin that still dwelled deep inside of you. Your sinful nature fought with your spiritual nature. In that internal warfare, My Grace was there for you and it was enough for everything that you had to deal with. My Power was made perfect in your weaknesses and it manifested when you were in your spirit, not in your flesh.

"Forgiving others and being forgiven by Me was very important, even though, many of you couldn't forgive yourselves for the things in your past. Some of you here today, tried to get Me to remember your past sins so that I may understand your past decisions, but I couldn't…I wouldn't. As long as you repented in your hearts, I threw that sin into the sea of forgetfulness. I do this because I love you. If I remember all your sins, even the ones you repented for, you would never get a fair chance. You would continue to carry the baggage of your past.

"When I made you, I made you with free will and just a little less than the angels in the Heavenly realm. I wanted the best for you, but you had to be willing to sacrifice the world and yourself for Me in order for Me to fulfill My promises to you.

"Jesus has chosen not to be here today for He knew there was nothing more He could say on your behalf. He has been at My right side pleading for each and every one of you, in spite of yourselves. You've all believed, but was it enough and where's it going to lead you to?"

The tall ominous figure finally makes his way up to the bailiff's desk. He leans over and whispers in the bailiff's ear. The bailiff looks at him for just a moment and approaches God. The bailiff whispers to God.

God ponders on the information provided by the bailiff. "We'll adjourn for 15 minutes," God said as He strikes the gavel.

"All rise," the bailiff says. Everyone stands. The presence of the Lord leaves the room.

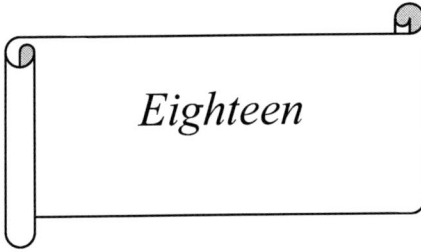

Eighteen

"*Y*ou may be seated," says the bailiff.

The souls sit down nervously whispering to each other. Now that God's presence has left the room, no one really knows what to do or even what to expect. Is this it for all those that are here? Is this the judgment they read, heard and learned about? Will they all make it into Heaven, in spite of the proceedings held earlier? Some of them had good reports of their lives. They walked and talked the faith in which they truly believed. Some had reports of hardship, trials and tribulations like none other, but they maintained their faith and their *Walk of Salvation* as God so keenly put it. There were some who had stories where they believed, but they didn't always follow His Word. And then there were those who just had their own agenda. They believed they loved God, but it was obvious that they also loved themselves and the ways of the world.

The one question still remained…*Was it enough to just believe?* God stated that believing was only that first step. All throughout the Bible it tells you that you just need to believe. If you believe, you will be saved. If you believe, you will have eternal life. If you believe, you will not perish. If you believe, if you believe, if you believe! Could that have misled them into thinking that belief was all it took and their actions did not matter? Was it enough to just believe?

"All rise," the bailiff says again. Everyone stands and all the whispering ceases.

God's presence reenters the courtroom. Once God's presence enters in, He nods to the bailiff.

The bailiff speaks. "He that shall endure until the end shall be saved. Souls, you may sit in the presence of the Almighty God." They all sit down.

"Some of you have endured and some of you have not," God said. "Nonetheless, your fate has been determined. You had an opportunity to know Me for yourself. You are people of the Christian church and were dedicated to some form of duty within the church. Was your heart in the work of the church or the work of the Lord? There is a difference. Was it about you, or was it about Me? Did you really love Me, or did you love you more? Before judgment is handed out, we have a witness who will speak and present something to you." He looks over to the witness who has made his way to the only empty chair in the front of the room. "You may proceed."

The witness stands and faces God. "Giving honor to God," he says as he bows before the Lord God and then turns to speak to the souls. "I know this may be a moment of uncertainty, but I ask for but a moment of your time. I've come to tell my story to all who may hear it. Before our Highest of the High leaves us, hear me out, for this is my testimony.

"You see, I too, as some of you have, once thought I could serve God and still maintain my own agenda. God gave me this identity and I knew He did a darn good job. I was and I am quite successful. You see, God gave me a musical gift and I was extremely good at it. As a matter of fact, I'm still good at what I do and that's because He never takes away our gifts. To this day, I am still the best musician who has ever existed. No one on earth has been able to out do what I've accomplished. I doubt if anyone ever will. I can sing the music. I can play the music, and more importantly, I compose the music. Am I full of myself? Maybe, but remember God made me this way just like He made you… that way." He frowns as he looks down on the souls.

"I made things happen that no one else could've ever done. The problem was, I got nothing for it. You hear me? I got nothing, absolutely nothing. So I decided since I didn't get what I deserve, I'll just take it. I mean, I went after what I thought I should have. I was entitled to it. Well…, things didn't work out as I had planned. To be more honest, and I do hate that word, *honest*, but I got a whole lot more than I bargained for.

"Now, I'm doing time for my theft and rebellion. I actually got the death penalty for my actions but God has not carried it out yet." All the souls in the room gasp at the thought that this is one of the souls that didn't make it, but came to tell them how bad it will be. Maybe he's here to tell them that they still have a chance and to not make the mistakes he made. The whispers between the souls start up again.

"But that's okay," the witness continues after hearing the murmuring as he walks back and forth, up and down the aisle. "You do the crime, you do the time. Only thing is…" he stops pacing and looks directly at them with such a menacing expression, "I don't plan on going down alone."

The souls look at him confused by his words.

"You see, a lot of you here and back on earth, are just like me. You like what I like and do what I do. You think no one can see your garbage just because the lid is closed."

The form of the witness begins to change, slowly and ever so slightly. The change is so subtle, the souls don't even notice. As this change is taking place, God and the bailiff depart from the courtroom. As they depart, angelic-like beings begin coming through the courtroom doors. Hundreds and hundreds of them, piling in one by one lining up along the back and side walls, lining up in all the aisles. They look at no soul. They focus on no particular thing or person. They just continue to pour in the room moving gracefully and with timed precision.

The souls are nervously looking around at all that's going on, trying to understand what's happening, and the witness grins and laughs. "But you know what?" The souls all turn to look back at this witness. "People tend to think they have more time than they actually have. It's always, *not today, I can do it tomorrow. I'll get saved tomorrow,* or *I'll do right tomorrow.* Of course, by all means, wait until tomorrow…please wait until tomorrow. Why do today, what you can do tomorrow?"

The witness continues to talk to the souls, moving back and forth across the front of the room, the only place where the angelic beings haven't come.

"All of you who think you can straddle the fence; who think you can live one way around the church and another way at your job, at your homes, around your friends… Well…I've come to tell you that there are two sides to every fence. No matter what people say you never really straddled the fence, you've actually jumped over. But on what side have you landed?

"You know who you are. And guess what, I know who you are. You see, the bailiff isn't the only one who knows the Word. It says in Revelation 3:15, '*I know your works; they are neither hot or cold. I would have preferred that you were hot or cold; but since you're lukewarm, I will spit you out of my mouth.'* Now what a horrible thing to say to someone. I would never say anything like that to you. You believe me?

"Just let me tell you one thing, God was so right when He said you can never serve two masters. You will hate one and love the other. No more accurate words have been said. Nope, you'll never be able to serve two masters, you're only serving one."

The witness begins to pull at his face. Something appears to be crawling all over it. He continues to pull and slap at his face. A serious transformation is going on right before their eyes. Everyone in the courtroom is horrified and now realizes who this witness must be. He didn't come there to give them any hope. He came to take them, but what about the angelic beings all over the place? Will they protect them? Is that why God had the angels come in while He and the bailiff left?

But something is happening with the angels. They are beginning to fly around the room almost as if circling the room and at such high speed. They move so fast but the air is not disturbed. There's no breeze from their movement, nothing stirs. This seems so impossible. The air is still, but they are moving faster and faster and faster. The souls also take notice of the transformation taking place in this thing that stands before them with his testimony, calling himself a witness. The tall ominous figure is a phony but he's no longer in the appearance of which he originally was. He has now become a tall grotesque figure, who appears to be severely beaten. There are gashes all over him. The gashes are so severe, his form looks completely distorted. The so-called witness's face becomes contorted as he continues to speak to all the souls. He's now yelling at the top of his lungs.

"You all are all questioning in your minds if believing was enough, well, guess what, *I Am...A Believer.*" He laughs once again and the menacing sound of it could curdle one's blood. He continues to yell. "*You Are Serving Me And Only Me. I Am Your Master. I'm...Your Master...of Death. I've been given the death penalty and I am here to share it with you. I welcome you to my side of the fence. Welcome...to HELL!*"

The souls begin to scream at satan's words and his laugh becomes deafening in their ears. But something else has happened. Souls are missing. Some of the souls have disappeared. The angelic beings have also disappeared. The beings that remain now show ghastly teeth that look as if they have been soaked in blood. Everything becomes clear as they realize their fate and start running around the room trying to get away from those things. It cannot be...but it has happened. God has judged the people of the church. But who was able to make it out?

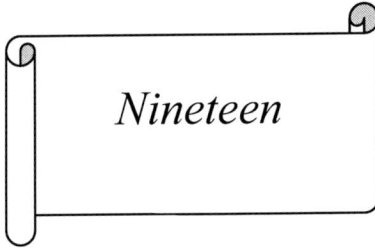

Nineteen

"*Jada*...Jada..."

"Do you think she can hear me?"

"You never can tell in these situations. Just keep..."

Jada hears voices and tries to open her eyes.

"Look, her eyes moved!"

"Jada...Jada...do you know where you are? Can you hear me?" says an unfamiliar voice. Her eyes flutter but she's not yet able to completely open them. Her eyelids are so heavy and she feels like she's floating.

"Jada...Jada...can you hear me?"

Now that voice was familiar, very familiar. Jada tries again to open her eyes and blinks to focus. There are a few strange and blurry images around her. She strains to see when she hears another familiar voice.

"Please Jada, wake up. We love you. I love you."

Jada tries with all that's in her to see. She finally opens her eyes to see Aaron and Maxine standing over her.

"Praise God, praise God. Hallelujah!" shouts Maxine. "Girl you had us scared. Thank you Jesus." Maxine bends down and hugs her, but makes sure she's very gentle. Aaron kisses her on the forehead.

Jada continues to look around past Maxine and Aaron, trying to understand what's going on. She notices that there are more people around her.

"Jada… honey, speak to me," Aaron said. "We're all here. We're here for you."

"Let her get her bearings," spoke the unfamiliar voice again. "She's been out for a couple of days so it's going to take a few moments."

Jada blinks repeatedly and her focus returns. She seems to be in an unfamiliar room. It looks like a hospital room. *What's happening? What's going on? Why would she be in a hospital?* She wonders as she tries to sit up.

"Oh no, young lady," the unfamiliar voice said as she gently pushes Jada down on her bed. "My name is Dr. Johnston. You were in an accident. So don't rush to sit up. Let me raise your head a little." Dr. Johnston pushes the button to raise the head section of Jada's bed to a position where she will not be tempted to move her head around. "Okay, this should be good. I'm going to leave for a minute, but I'll be back.

"I've allowed all these people to be here for you and they've been praying for you day and night. I was so inspired by their faith in God and their love for you that I attended some of their prayer vigils. I must say, it was spiritually uplifting for me and I really needed that as a physician. But enough about me, this is all about you. Everyone was given permission to be here around the clock, just in case you woke up anytime soon. Good thing it was soon."

Dr. Johnston looks up, looking at no thing in particular. "I'm sure someone else had a hand in this." She shakes her head to focus back on Jada. Dr. Johnston smiles at Jada. "I better go, I'm sure you all have some catching up to do. Just take it easy and don't rush anything. Your friends will explain everything to you. Don't let her get up," she says to the others and then leaves the room.

"Girl, don't you ever scare me like that again," Maxine said. "I don't think I've ever prayed so hard." Tears start falling down her face.

"What...happened? Why am I here...in a hospital?" Jada asked.

"I'll let someone else answer that." Maxine steps back and allows Aaron to talk to her.

"Hey sweetie. How are you feeling?" Aaron asked. "You were in ..."

Jada looks beyond Aaron and sees James and Ellie Addams. James has a bandage above his right eye. But there are more people in the room. There's Peaches with her sons, Joshua and Jacob Wright. Even Pastor Jon Devine is here. Oh no, over in the corner crying, is Trina with Mychal trying to calm her down. Even Ms. Che Che is here. "Am I… dreaming?" she asked not really hearing Aaron.

"Oh no baby, you're definitely not dreaming," Aaron said. "You're in the hospital. You were almost hit by a car."

"What!" She thinks about it for a moment and looks over at James. "Did you try to hit me, Deacon James?"

He and Ellie glance at each other in amazement and then move up to Jada's bed. "No way Sister Jada," James said. "It was not like that at all. You ran…wait…how did you know it was me? It was all so fast."

"You were going to say, I ran out into the street where you hit and killed me… yourself and LJ," Jada said. "I did not see your car coming until it was too late. You hit me! You killed me! How could you do something like that?" Jada stops, realizing what she's saying. "But…if you killed me, how…did the paramedics revive me? But that wouldn't explain your family." Jada rubs her head and tries to remember what happened. She feels the bandage on her head and starts to check her legs, her arms, to see if she's intact. She gives a sigh of relief. "What is going on?"

"Is that how you remember the accident?" Pastor Devine asked.

"You know, I'm not sure anymore what I remember Pastor…but Deacon James, did you or did you not hit me?"

"No Sister Jada, I didn't, but I almost did. You jumped out in front of my car. It's a good thing LJ saw you. I was able to hit the brakes. That's how I got this bruise on my head. I hit the brakes so hard my head hit the steering wheel. It was Aaron who grabbed you and pulled you back where you both fell onto the curb. You came down real hard and hit your head on the edge of the curb and have been in a coma since then."

"A coma? You mean, I was never dead? I didn't die?"

"No honey, you never died. I will never allow anything to happen to you that's within my power," Aaron said.

"Then it was all a dream?"

"All what was a dream, honey?" Ms. Che Che asked.

"Lord have mercy," Maxine said. "Girl ain't no telling what you may have dreamed for the past few days."

Jada begins to sit up slowly and Aaron jumps to help her up. "Don't rush it Jada, you heard what the doctor said."

"You all will not believe it. It was so real. It's hard for me to believe it didn't happen. But the more I think about it, I know exactly what it was." She turns towards James and Ellie. "Deacon, like I said, you, me and LJ were killed in that car accident. Ellie was the sole survivor and her prognosis was not good. Even Jacob died."

"Hey," Jacob said. "How did I get in there? I was no where near the accident."

"I know Jay, that's true, but remember when I overheard you and Josh talking…arguing about those boys that tried to jump you?"

"What?" Peaches said. "Who tried to jump you? When was all this?"

Joshua and Jacob lower their heads.

"I thought about you two a lot after that," Jada said. "That's probably why you were included in my dream. But in actuality, your life was needed for what God needed me to see. But I saw God, really I did. I was there, in the presence of God."

Pastor Devine smiles. "Wow. That must've been some dream. You know sometimes God has a way of telling you things through your dreams. He may use it as a way to talk to you when you don't hear Him 'cause you aren't in your spirit long enough or even at all. He may use it to give you direction or insight. He has even used it as a way to warn us.

"But the most important thing is you need to make sure it's of God. You can do that by just asking Him to show you a sign, give you confirmation. You can even name your sign, but this is only possible if you have a relationship with Him and regularly pray or meditate with Him in your spirit. Our connection to God is through the spirit. If all this has taken place, you must take heed to His message before it's too late."

"Oh Pastor, I know it was God. This could not have been anyone but God. Not only did He talk to me, but there we were, all of us at our judgment. We were giving an account of our life here on earth.

"Then there was satan who showed up like he was trying to help us, and then all these angels appeared and then they…" Jada looks around at everyone who are looking at her with such puzzled looks. "I know I am rambling on and on, and it's so hard for you to picture it, but God has given me another chance guys. I've never been so sure about anything as I am about this."

She looks at Maxine and begins to cry. "Girl, I've done you so wrong in more ways than I can name. I cannot believe I was trippin' on you like that. You've been my girl since forever, and I became so self-absorbed that I completely blocked you out. You tried to get me focused, but I lashed out against you instead. I'm sorry for trying to make you choose between God and me. I was so wrong for that.

"You too Trina. I treated you like you was my servant and like I was so much better than you. And no matter what I did to you, you stuck by my side. I love you for that." Trina had stopped crying but now after hearing this, she's crying all over again.

Jada smiles and turns towards Aaron. "Aaron, you saved my life in more ways than you know. I remember the argument we had before the accident and you were right. Everything you said was absolutely right. Don't you dare feel guilty about what happened. It was necessary for me and it was all part of God's plan to save my life. I will always be thankful to you for making the stand in our life for what's right. Through this whole ordeal, my eyes have been opened.

"Pastor…Minister Peaches, I even took advantage of you two and I'm so sorry. Everybody, please, I need to ask for your forgiveness. I've been rude, mean, arrogant, insensitive and intolerable. Ms. Che Che, you've been such a mother figure for me since my mother died. I've always appreciated you and I think you're the only one here I have not wronged."

"That's because you know better. You know what side your bread is buttered on," Ms. Che Che said as everyone laughed.

"But you know Pastor, what I experienced was no dream. It was a vision. It was a vision of my judgment. My own judgment before God." Jada pauses for a moment as she reflects back on the memory of her dream, her vision. Tears fall in full force. "I need everyone to stand around my bed please, and hold hands."

Everyone does as Jada asks. She looks around her bed at each of them as she talks. "When I'm out of here, I want to do something really special. I have to do something special. I need you all to come over to my place so I can tell you all about this vision. I have a feeling it's not just for me. I need to tell you the complete details. You all played a major role in it, and I love each of you so much."

They all glance at each other from time to time while listening to Jada. All the women are crying. None of them have ever seen her this way before. It's obvious that something serious happened while she was in that coma.

She continues to speak through her flood of tears. "God used my coma to help me to see inside myself. To see what you all have been seeing and trying to tell me. Every one of you has tried to help me live the life I should've lived as a *'proclaimed'* Christian, but I didn't see it. No matter what you said or did, I didn't see it. God had to literally take me out, to bring me in."

"It looks like God had to knock you out, literally, to get your attention," Ms. Che Che said.

"Yeah, and she's got a big bump on the head to prove it. Heyyyyy!" Trina says as she does her dance.

Everyone in the room laughs at that, even Jada. Aaron wipes the tears from Jada's face as she begins to gently rub her head. "You know what?" Jada said. This bruise will always be a reminder of God's message to me. He helped me to see and understand what this Christian walk is all about. I am making a vow to God. That not *one day*…but from *this day* on, I will be a hearer *and* a doer of His Word. I will look to the hills for my help. I will acknowledge God in everything I do. I will allow my flesh to die, so that God can come forth through me. For now I know, it's not about me. It's all about Him. Everyone, please pray with me." Jada closes her eyes, but holds her head up as if looking up at God, Himself.

Conclusion
Chapter Questions

1) Even though there are different classes of music, are there really only two types of music; one that glorifies God and one that glorifies satan? Why or Why not?

2) Is it okay to listen to Gospel and secular music? Is it okay to buy, watch, and attend concerts for both Gospel and secular music? Are both types of music acceptable for Christians? Why or why not?

3) The Judge stated that music has a way of influencing you. He said one feeds your spirit and one feeds your flesh. When you sing and listen to secular music, is there any difference in the way you feel compared to when you sing and listen to Gospel music?

4) Jada felt as long as she sang secular music with good taste, it would be alright. This kind of music is called inspirational music. Is this alright for a Christian? Why?

5) Is there anything wrong with going to a club and church on the same day? Is it acceptable as a Christian to hang out at the club for some fun? Is it hypocritical to party at the club and be a worshipper of God?

6) Since Jada was a nightclub singer as well as the lead vocalist for the church choir, was it acceptable or hypocritical to sing at both places and does it really matter? Should there be a difference between an individual's personal and Christian life?

7) Should Maxine have gone to see her best friend, Jada, perform at the Wild Card? Why or why not? Was Maxine right for taking the position she did about visiting the Wild Card?

8) Was Maxine too 'stuffy' as Jada called it? Was she being self-righteous or truly concerned? What does 'being religious' mean?

9) Maxine felt as though she had to get Jada back on the right course. As a Christian, is it your job to steer a loved one who is also a believer back in the right direction if you feel they have gone astray? How would you do that?

10) Should Pastor Jon Devine have confronted Jada about her double life of singing in the club and in the church? Was it the pastor's business what she did in her private life?

11) What do you believe your pastor would say about members singing and hanging out in nightclubs? Is it the pastor's responsibility to confront those who do?

12) What does, 'Don't be so heavenly bound, that you are no earthly good' mean to you?

13) The Addams family played the lottery faithfully. Is gambling acceptable? What difference does it make? What harm is there in buying tickets, rolling dice, playing cards, picking odds, etc.?

14) While at the club, Mychal told Jada he could not tell Christians from Non-Christians. Is this true in your surroundings? Is there or should there be a difference between the two? Where should the line be drawn?

15) Peaches, Maxine, Jada, and the bailiff quoted scriptures from the Bible to prove their points. How important is reading the Bible? How important is studying the Bible or is reading and studying pretty much the same?

16) Trina and James said they did not read the Bible because they trust the words of their pastor. Should church members just accept what the pastor preaches? Is this enough or is there more they should do for themselves?

17) Joshua and Jacob were faced with some pretty mean characters. Should they have confided in someone about what was going on? Would it make you *soft* to tell on someone? Would it make you *soft* to walk away from a fight or is it best to handle it right then and there? If you were in their shoes, how would you have handled it?

18) Trina told her friends that they should not argue God's Word. Is there a problem with arguing with another about the Bible? Is it appropriate to argue about someone's different interpretations of the Bible? What if someone doesn't believe in the Bible? Are there any repercussions for arguing?

19) Aaron became saved and began to question his entire life as well as his relationship with Jada. Was Aaron wrong in trying to change their relationship? Was Aaron moving too fast with his decisions or should he have waited a while before discussing it with her?

20) The Judge gave the souls *'food for thought'* when it came to drinking and smoking. There is no specific scripture in the Bible about smoking. Since the Bible does not address smoking by name (such as other acts like; fornicating, drinking, stealing, etc.), how can it be a sin?

21) If we do something to our body which can result in harm, would that be considered a sinful act? What are some harmful things people do to their bodies all the time? Are any of those a sin? Why or why not?

22) During LJ's judgment, he was considered innocent in the eyes of the Lord. What made him innocent? Are there

people you believe God considers innocent and unaccountable for sin?

23) Do you think it was easy for Maxine and Jada to live celibate lives and why was it important? Why did Jada give in to fornication and Maxine didn't? Most people want to test the waters, is that alright? What's the purpose of continuing celibacy if you have met your future husband or wife?

24) Are you still saved, even if you continue to do what you know is sinful? What does the following scripture mean? Matthew 24:13, *But he that endures to the end, shall be saved.* 'Endure what? What is 'saved'?

25) Did you recognize yourself in any of the characters? What would you have done differently? What are your likes and/or dislikes about any of the characters?

26) Why do you think the author chose '2Chronicles 7:11-16, 19-20' for the Introduction and how does it relate to the story?   Also, how does the chapter title, relate to the message of the book?

27) A couple of references were made to God never taking away the gifts He gives us. How true is that, or is it true?

If you have more questions to add to the discussion or would help with self-discovery, use the following additional space.

28)

29)

30)

Be on the lookout for these newly published plays and skits.
All of the author's writings are part of her 'dramedy' (drama + comedy) style.

Author - Playwright
Cheryl Patton-Bronson

*Teen Trilogy: Mid-length play of a rebellious teen basketball star; a devoted praise dancer led astray by a relationship with a local boy; and a drug addicted young man on the run. They all run into big trouble but reach out to the only One that can save them before it's too late.

**A Child Is Born: Short skit on the birth of Jesus as it's written in the book of Matthews in the New Testament. Perfect for children ages five through ten.

**If Jesus Was Born Today: Phenomenal full length play depicting the birth, life, death, and resurrection of Jesus Christ in the twenty-first century.

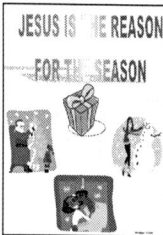

**Jesus Is The Reason For The Season: Skit regarding high school students trying to celebrate Christmas while helping a fellow student understand the true meaning of Christmas. But a non-believing teacher is trying to get in the way.

*It's Not Too Late: Full length play about teen issues of sex, disease, humiliation, and abortion. A combination of characters from 'Teen Trilogy' and 'Jesus Is The Reason For The Season'.

*One Day This Day: Full length play of God's judgment on the people of the church. A comedic and insightful play which inspired the novel of the same name.

These plays can be purchased separately or collectively.

*"*Words from the Spirit Collection I*

Christian Plays"

or

**"*Words from the Spirit Collection II*

Holiday Play & Skits"

Write us a review by telling us what you think about this book. Just visit us @ www.4yourspirit.com and fill out the review form. Check out our Christian Superstore and get an additional 10% off the already discounted prices of all your biblical and spiritual needs.

One Day…This Day!

Cheryl Patton-Bronson

GIVE THE GIFT OF One Day…This Day! TO YOUR FAMILY, FRIENDS AND COLLEAGUES

Use This Convenient Order Form For Additional Copies

_____ copies of One Day…This Day @ $19.95 each $_____
Shipping and handling @$4.60 $_____
Each additional book @$1.95 $_____
(Order 5 or more books, - FREE SHIPPING)
Illinois residents add 9% sales tax $_____
Total Amount $_____

Payment must accompany orders. Allow up to 1 week for delivery.

My check or money order for $_____ is enclosed.

Please charge my ☐ VISA ☐ MC

NAME_____

ORGANIZATION_____

ADDRESS_____

CITY/STATE/ZIP_____

PHONE_____EMAIL_____

CARD #_____

EXP. DATE_____CIV#_____

SIGNATURE_____

MAIL/FAX ORDER FORM
MAKE CHECKS PAYABLE TO:
4 YOUR SPIRIT PRODUCTIONS
P.O. BOX 201718
CHICAGO, ILLINOIS 60620-1718
FAX# 773-304-1933
WRITE YOUR COMMENTS ON BACK OF FORM

TELL US WHAT YOU THINK ABOUT
"ONE DAY…THIS DAY"
and receive a free gift.

_____

_____

_____

_____

_____

_____

_____

_____

_____

_____

_____

_____